MURDERED in MEDINA

... and other human interest stories

Copyright © 2005 by William McCarty

All rights reserved. No part of this book shall be reproduced or transmitted in any form or by any means, electronic, mechanical, magnetic, photographic including photocopying, recording or by any information storage and retrieval system, without prior written permission of the publisher. No patent liability is assumed with respect to the use of the information contained herein. Although every precaution has been taken in the preparation of this book, the publisher and author assume no responsibility for errors or omissions. Neither is any liability assumed for damages resulting from the use of the information contained herein.

This is a work of fiction. Names, characters, places, and incidents either are the product of the author's imagination or are used fictitiously. Any resemblance to actual events or locales or persons, living or dead, is entirely coincidental.

ISBN 0-7414-2776-1

Published by:

INFINITY
PUBLISHING.COM

1094 New DeHaven Street, Suite 100
West Conshohocken, PA 19428-2713
Info@buybooksontheweb.com
www.buybooksontheweb.com
Toll-free (877) BUY BOOK
Local Phone (610) 941-9999
Fax (610) 941-9959

Printed in the United States of America

Printed on Recycled Paper

Published September 2005

Table of Contents

Murdered in Medina 1
Dime Daisies 6
Alias O'Lynque 8
Blue Gray Veteran 12
"Filter, Flavor-" 15
Chippewa Fleet 18
The Beachcomber 22
Pfundstein's Folly 26
Petty Girl Painter 30
Ace Brigode and the Birth of Radio 33
Dick Booth 41
Blaze In 46
Busy Sky 50
Wall Street Mink 54
Baby Ace 57
Eddie Paul 59
Medina, New York 63
Batman 66
Tony 71
Jockey Willie 75
Canary Yellow 79
The Candy Maker 83
Kip 87
Story Hour 93

Introduction

These short stories about Medina County, Ohio people were originally written for the Medina *County Leader Post* from 1957 to 1960 by Bill McCarty, then Managing Editor of the weekly newspaper.

Three of them, *Murdered in Medina*, *The Chippewa Fleet* and *Medina, NY*, won an annual *Best in Ohio*, first place award presented by the *Ohio Newspaper Association*. A lost story, *Writer Teaches School*, won the honor in 1960 and placed third in the National Editorial Association competition that same year.

McCarty left Medina in 1960 to become a career Chamber of Commerce executive in Ohio, Iowa and Florida. He retired in 1987. He and his family loved the little community of Medina and were involved in many of its small-town social activities, including the *Medina Masquers* and the *Junior Chamber of Commerce*.

This book is dedicated to Medina friends who made their lives interesting, fun and exciting while they lived there.

MURDERED IN MEDINA
and other
HUMAN INTEREST STORIES
By Bill McCarty

The Medina County Courthouse
Then and Now

Murdered in Medina

The information contained in this story is based upon actual court records and recollections of people whose grandparents lived in Medina County at the time of the event. Dates, names, and places are actual and accurate. The recorded sequence of events, before and after the trial, no longer exists. No books or documents published on the history of Medina, or Medina County, include this murder story in their texts.

The Cleveland Sheppard murder case is still a hot subject whenever party talk turns to the more gruesome aspects of our society. However, in time the names of Doctor Sam, Sauk Donaceau, William Corrigan, Samuel R. Gerber, and Mayor Spencer Hauk will be lost to our memories.

If you don't believe this to be true, let us refer to an equally despicable crime that was committed in Medina on July 2, 1863. The local murder must have had the same sensational impact on people of that generation as the Sheppard story had on ours.

Shubal Coy was a stock dealer. He, his wife, and young son lived at 227 South Elmwood Street, Medina, in a modest home that is standing today. Coy regularly drove cattle into Cleveland where he received large sums of money, which he carried back home with him. He generally arrived late at night.

F.F.Streeter was Coy's best friend. In fact, he knew the family so intimately that the formalities of casual relationship were uncalled for. If Streeter came to visit, and he did so regularly, he walked into the home as if it were his own.

On July 2, 1863, Coy made one of his regular trips to the Lake City. It was his last. Mrs. Coy had a premonition about that fateful day. She told one of her neighbors that morning that she had a feeling something awful was going to happen. It did.

Coy arrived home late. It was after dark. He took his horse to the livery stable behind the house and then entered the dwelling and went directly to his bedroom. He was tired from the day's journey. What really happened after Coy reached his room will never be known.

The next morning all was quiet at the Coy home. Too quiet. The ominous heavy, hot July air was as still as the dead of night.

A neighbor called at the house to chat with Mrs. Coy. No one answered her knock at the door. That was unusual. She had not seen anyone leave. Mrs. Coy and her young son seldom left the house for long. Perhaps they were down the street, better check the livery. She had heard Shubal come home last night. The horse is here...I wonder? Did I hear scuffling and the loud voices of two men last night? Is there something wrong?

She returned to the house, cautiously opened the door, and entered the living room. Nothing out of order here. Shubal are you home? Silence, hot, dead, muggy, damp, empty silence.

She went into the kitchen. Nothing. Should she go upstairs? Something urged her to do so. Now she was smelling something. Smoke! Was the house on fire? Quickly. In the back, in the back! The bedroom, the bedroom!

The sight she saw when she entered the room was one she never forgot. Blood was everywhere! Shubal, his wife, and little son lay in grotesque death. They had been cut and slashed. The room had been ransacked. The neighbor went screaming into the street.

The investigation that followed disclosed that the money Coy had received for his stock had been stolen. It was suggested that the killer murdered Mrs. Coy and her son, then secreted himself in a closet to wait on Coy to arrive. In any event, he tried to cover up his crime by setting the house on fire. In his haste to leave, he had failed to get the fire properly started, it went out before the room, and the crime scene, was consumed in flame.

When Streeter was told his friends had been murdered he came to the house and wept openly. It appeared the triple slaying was a horrible surprise to him. Soon after his visit, he disappeared. Several weeks later, bloodstained money was spent in several cities west of Medina. Streeter was identified as the man who had passed the stained bills.

On September 17, 1863, Samuel Bradley filed an affidavit of investigation. Streeter was arrested and jailed by constable N.W. Piper. An initial hearing was postponed until September 9. On the seventh and eighth, twenty witnesses were subpoenaed to sit on the grand jury. Streeter pleaded not guilty to the charge of murder and was returned to jail. A formal indictment was prepared and filed on November 13. Streeter was accused of "unlawfully, feloniously, purposely and of deliberate and premeditated intent, cutting and stabbing Shubal Coy who died of a mortal wound 1½ inches long to a depth of five inches." Court records do not mention his wife or son. Trial was set for November 24.

On November 16, thirty-six citizens were called to be examined for a 12-man jury. Wadsworth Township was called upon to furnish eleven citizens, Sharon-eight, Granger-twelve, Hinkley-four, and Medina-one. When impaneled, Wadsworth had four persons on the jury, Sharon had five, and Granger had three. The court records are not clear as to whom the 12th juror was, his name is listed but he was not one of the original 36 called.

The Honorable Stevenson Burke, one of the judges of the 4th Judicial District, presided. Stephen B. Woodward was the prosecutor for the State. H. G. Blake was the court-appointed defense attorney. When the trial began November 24 the jurors were taken to the scene of the crime. They were asked to return to the courtroom November 28. After deliberation, the jury retired to study the evidence. Streeter was indicted on three counts (not detailed in official court records). He was found not guilty on counts one and three. The jury did find him guilty of the unknown second count.

When the verdict was announced, an immediate request was made for a new trial on the grounds that there has been insufficient evidence to warrant the finding. The request was overruled. The judge declared that Streeter would hang on Friday, February 26, 1864 between the hours of 10 AM and 4 PM, "herein provided he pay cost of prosecution." Would they have hung him if he had refused?

February 26 was a big day in the history of Medina. Early in the morning the square began to fill with people. Hitching posts were difficult to find where wagons and buggies could be parked.

The hanging took place not far from where the City Park is today. After the prisoner was pronounced dead, and there was nothing more to be seen, everyone returned to the town square to talk the matter over, pro and con. Was he guilty? Some believed he was not, others were sure that he was.

No one living today was a witness to the Streeter murder trial or hanging. Very few people even know it happened. The only visible evidence remaining is a worn tombstone in a small grave covered with myrtle. The monument, on Route 192 near the Medina Infirmary, states in timeworn hand carved letters, "Shubal Coy murdered in Medina."

Dime Daisies

Every Friday morning Mike and Sarah Bardy, age two and six, eagerly await the arrival of the postman who delivers a letter that contains a bright new dime for each of them. They save the dimes until Christmas time to buy presents for their friends.

Getting coins in the mail is big news to the youngsters but it would not be especially newsworthy here except the way they are used to express a grandmother's love, and to teach the children more about the world in which they live.

Grandmother Bardy shares her Cleveland home with a daughter who is an artist. Each week the dimes are worked into a cartoon that either expresses the season of the year, an object lesson or a word of greeting. Sometimes the art also includes a little verse because artist Phyllis Greene had, at one time, written verses for a greeting card company.

Phyllis even took photographs of the children so that her drawings of them would be accurate. Typical of the cartoons received was a sketch of them blowing bubbles. The bubbles were real dimes. A Halloween sketch received just before the holiday had dimes for pumpkins. Marjorie Bardy, the youngster's mother, selected the "kids in a wagon" sketch as her favorite because the likeness of the children was so well done.

The Bardys live in Medina. Franklin, the man of the household, is a schoolteacher in Strongsville. "My mother started the dime-a-week habit and it just grew. The children would sure be disappointed if there was an interruption of mail service," he said.

This spring, when early flowers first appeared through the late winter snow, dime daisies arrived at the Bardy home to herald the coming of the new season. Later, a November flower cartoon reminded the children of the coming of winter. Grandmother Bardy wrote, "These posies bloom in November. They come to you to say grandma likes to remember her kiddies this way." Last week the youngsters received a drawing of a Christmas tree with dimes for decoration.

A lesson in thrift, a simple story of the changing seasons and, most of all, an expression of a grandmother's love for her family are represented by the dime cartoons.

The youngsters will remember their Friday fun when the postman arrives, long after they have children of their own.

Alias O'Lynque

You can meet all kinds of people in Brunswick, and until last Thursday evening I thought I had. That was before I met Bob Vokes of 174 Huntington Circle.

Bob is the kind of fellow that does not talk much about his hobby with neighbors, although he is willing to do so. He volunteered to subject himself to this reporter's questions. Two hours later I was on my way back to the shop with pages of notes, none of which I could understand very well.

Bob is a cryptoanalyst. A cryptoanalyst is one who, without knowledge of the key or the system, solves cryptograms. In the event you still do not know what I am talking about, a cryptogram is a communication prepared in cipher or code; more specifically applied to "Aristocrats." An "Aristocrat" in this instance is a monoalphabetic or simple substitution cipher in which plain text word lengths are retained. Did I leave you back there 10 lines or so?

To make a short story shorter, and perhaps a wee bit clearer, Vokes is a member of the *American Cryptogram Association* in Greenfield, Mass. This group pursues the hobby of solving word puzzles, an aversion for solving secret writing. They work with ciphers and codes, which are not to be confused with each other. You will not learn that difference here because the details were over my head.

For the record, it took me an hour to find Vokes house after dark in a driving rain and I got soaked knocking on the doors of his neighbors, Voight and Varney! It is Vokes, dummy. When I did get to what I thought was the right place, an attractive lady welcomed me in with, "Mr. McCarty, I would like you to meet my husband Bob O'Lynque." Confused?

Bob Volkes was "Bob O'Lynque." Mrs. Vokes was "Missy Link." By this time, I was catching on. These code names were in keeping with Bob's cryptogram hobby I thought. With a smile that meant I was getting wise, I asked, "And what do your code names mean?" "Absolutely nothing at all," was the reply. "We just use a nom de plume for the fun of it."

Bob and his eccentric pals do have a practical purpose in our society. The armed forces send messages in code and cipher and these specialists would be valuable to call upon in case of conflict. One of the present members of the *ACA* broke the Japanese code in World War II. Cipher clerks and cryptoanalysts are used by the military in war and peace. Diplomatic messages are exchanged in code.

According to Vokes, anyone could be trained as a cipher clerk because he has a codebook to refer to when he receives a message or sends one. The analyst, on the other hand, breaks codes without any knowledge of the senders system. Similarly, he tries to develop a system that is difficult to decipher by anyone except the person, or persons, for whom it is intended. It appeared obvious that anyone could make a code that someone else could not solve. This assumption was wrong, according to Vokes. "The system would have to be practical," he said. "After all, the person to whom it was sent would have to know how to break it and in such a case you would soon learn it was "old stuff" to others.

"To be practical, such a system must contain certain essentials. It must be suitable for telegraphic transmission and it should be rapidly decipherable by the recipient for whom it is intended. It should not permit more than one interpretation and if an omission or error appears in the text, it should not affect the complete message, " he explained.

Bob said that there are other basic rules a message should go by, but they all add up to being simple for your friends and difficult for your enemies. No practical cipher system has ever been invented that has not been broken, although the use of ciphers goes back as far as man's history is recorded.

The *ACA* has about 500 members all over the world but only two local chapters now exist, one in Rochester, NY and one in New York City. A third chapter is being formed in Washington, DC.

A doctor from Mississippi, a writer from Columbus, Ohio and a chap from Burton, Ohio organized the *ACA* in 1923. In 1932, the fellow from Burton started a bi-monthly periodical, which became the official publication of the *ACA*. The publication contains, among other things, various types of cryptograms ranging from the easiest "Aristocrats" to the more difficult "Vigeners," "Portas," and "Beauforts." It contained at least 50 puzzles, each of which has it's own key to solution. Experts can work the easy ones in a matter of minutes; the same experts may require many hours to solve the difficult ones.

A history published by the *ACA* this month points out that there is much more to cryptology than knowing the devices employed, suggesting "it keeps the mind occupied in clear sound thinking and prevents the individual from musing on the less pleasant things of life."

Bob is a cost analyst for *the Pittsburgh Steamship Division of the U.S. Steel Company* in Cleveland. He is not a crackpot, as evidenced by his occupation. He was the 1957 president of *ACA* and has been interested in word puzzles for close to 30 years.

Blue Gray Veteran

There are not many Blue Gray Veterans alive. Rudy Linek is one of the two or three in Medina County. He lives on Route 303 in Brunswick. The old veteran of the Spanish American War and the Philippine Insurrection was born on April 13, 1880. He came to Brunswick from Cleveland in 1936.

Rudy is proud as a billygoat of his four years of military service many years ago. In memory of his fallen shipmates and buddies, he rarely misses a Memorial Day or Fourth of July celebration. He wears the uniform he bought in 1904.

Rudy enlisted in the Navy in 1898 when trouble with Spain was brewing. He joined a volunteer company of Cleveland, Cincinnati, St. Paul, and St. Louis boys.

There was no such thing as a draft in those days. Every man went off to war because he wanted to go. There were no bonuses, war risk insurance, vocational training, or hospitalization. Sixty-one percent of the enlistees saw foreign service and 74 percent were sons of Civil War Veterans.

Rudy trained for shipboard duty at Mare Island up the coast 30 miles from San Francisco. After three months of basic training, he was assigned to the crew of the *Indiana* that headed for Cuba. The *Indiana*, America's first battleship, joined our new fleet in the blockage of the Spanish island.

Rudy's *Indiana* was one of the battleships that bottled up the Spanish fleet in Santiago Bay. By day, the larger battlewagons would lie off shore in a wide arch guarding the harbor. At night they would close in and, using a figure-eight maneuver, take turns pointing their guns and searchlights through the bay opening at the Spanish ships anchored near the shore.

Rudy remembers how we tried to sink one of our own ships in the channel so the Spanish fleet could not get out. The sinking was not a complete success but it did force the enemy to leave the harbor one boat at a time. As they did so, our ships would sink them or drive them on to beaches. The war ended soon thereafter.

Adventure was not over for Rudy. Russia and China started a fight and he was assigned to an expedition ship, which had been converted to a gunboat and was heading for China. The salty old veteran has pictures of the boat; its name was the *Vicksburg*. Winter caught up with the *Vicksburg* at Neuchwang, China. There, coolies built a cover to protect its crew from the weather. The faded snapshot Rudy carries shows the ship anchored in Neuchwang Harbor. With the protective cover it looks like a floating quonset hut.

All through the war, our friend wore two badges on his undershirt that looked like "Willkie" buttons. One was the picture of his mother and the other a picture of his sweetheart. He still has them. The celluloids are still in excellent shape except the brass backs have tarnished. "Want to know why they are green?" He asked. "Well, they went with me everywhere. When I went overboard, they went too. The salt water didn't do them much good."

When his four-year hitch was over Rudy returned to Cleveland and married his sweetheart. He became a carpenter and worked at the trade until 1935 when he bought a 64-acre farm on the southeast corner of Route 303 and 22 in Brunswick Township.

"Here's a funny thing," Rudy said. "My deed read 64-acres more or less. When I sold this place a few weeks back they found out it had 72.98 acres. All that time I only paid taxes on the 64."

The Mrs. passed away a few years back and Rudy is now renting the 131-year-old house he lives in until he can find a place to go. He will tell you life has been good to him. His farm did well. Actually, he did not farm too long. He learned there was good money in dairy cattle. He kept a big herd.

Rudy belongs to the *General George A. Garrison Spanish American Post 4* headquarters in Cleveland. He was commander of it in 1917. Of the 56 commanders listed in the Post's roster of last year, there are only 13 still living. Yes, life was good to Rudy and he appreciated it. At 78 years of age, he stands as erect as a young athlete. He is alert and keenly aware of the world around him as well as the world that has passed.

He has one regret. He never had a son. He would have liked to have passed his rich heritage on to a boy who could venture into this wide world as he did 60 years ago.

"Filter, Flavor-"

"You get a lot with a Marlboro, filter, flavor, flip top box!" Ever wonder how the guys and dolls get the singing commercial assignments you hear by the score on radio and television?

Mary Davis, 645 Oak Street Medina, is a singing commercial artist. She sang her first one in February and will do some more before the year is over.

Mary, a graduate of Medina 10 years ago, sang with the school "Starduster" band for four years. She now sings with Floyd Soward's band of Lodi at VFW dances, proms, and private parties. One evening a few months ago Soward's band was playing for a private party in Cleveland. Mary sang a couple of numbers.

A party guest introduced himself and asked if she would like to try commercial recording. "Meet me at the Cinecraft Studios in Cleveland tomorrow and we will see if we can work something out," the ad agent said. The next day Mary had a baby-sitter watch over her two daughters while she made the trip to Cleveland.

At the studio, she was introduced to a combo of musicians who would do the background music for an animated television cartoon for which Mary would supply the voice. The combo consisted of a bass, vibraharp, and snare drums.

In addition to the musicians, Mary, the agency man, two engineers, and a director were on hand for the session. The commercial was to be 20-seconds long. Mary and the combo members were briefed on what the cartoon was all about so they could get the feel of the assignment; it would feature dancing telephones.

Lyrics for the commercial were furnished along with sheet music. Mary does not read music but she has a good ear. It did not take long for her to get the rhythm as written. Diction and time were the main problems of the day. One word, "Ohio," often came out "A-hi-a" and this called for repeats of the recording. The 20-seconds of time had to be precise; it was easy to be off a second one way or the other.

The recordings were done on tape. After each tape was made the engineers would play them back and the director would suggest diction, tone, or pitch correction. The session was four hours and 14 tapes long!

During a coffee break at 5pm the director and engineers picked out the three best "takes" and then the whole group settled down to critique their work. Finally, one tape was chosen as best. The engineers made a transcription record. Then it was ready for radio and television use.

Two weeks later thousands of radio and television listeners were hearing Mary sing, "Give your home a gay new ring for spring. Call Ohio Bell."

What does a singing commercial ad singer get paid? It depends. If you are a top star in the music field, you can name your own price. If you are a good singer without television or radio recognition, you get "union scale."

"You are paid whether the audition tape is used or not, which is fortunate since many of the tapes end up on the cutting room floor," Mary said. "Agencies will come up with an idea, make up tapes and then try to sell them to advertisers or their agents. If they are not bought it's the agency's loss not the artist's," she pointed out.

Is there a future in the ad making business for Mary? Probably not. The pay is good but the work is not steady. If the agencies like your voice then you are on call, beyond that there are no guarantees.

Mary also worked on a 60-minute commercial for Ohio Bell but this one did not "take." It will be used but another singer has the assignment. She also worked out the "bugs" in a Manner's Big Boy commercial that was so difficult some of the lyrics had to be rewritten. It was sent to New York for a professional singer to cut. "I always liked music," Mary said, "I do it as a hobby."

"Don't let her kid you," her husband Bill interjected, "We like the money. It's a paying hobby and that's the best kind."

Chippewa Fleet

If you are a person with a keen sense of observation, you have probably noticed sailboats with the picture of a *Shooting Star*, a *Snipe*, or just the letter *Y* on the mainsail. Usually these markings are accompanied by large numbers such as *368* or *121*. A sailboat enthusiast will bend your ear for as long as you will listen if you ask him, or her, what these markings mean. You can see these small craft on Chippewa Lake almost any nice day when there is a pleasant breeze blowing.

The *Y,* the *Snipe* and the *Shooting Star Comets,* as they are known in the trade, are class designations of sailboats. The number indicates they are registered with the official racing association. Generally speaking, a low number indicates its owner joined the association while it was still young. The art of sailing is anything but new. Books on the subject say it was learned 5000 years ago.

The *Chippewa Lake Yacht Club* has a fleet of 21 boats. Of these, the *Y* class is the largest with ten. There are five *Snipes,* two *Lightenings,* one *Pistol* and, pardon the expression, three outboards. The sailboat owner looks at an outboard like a child looks at a wasp. They are OK in their place, preferable at a distance.

Y owners were out in force two Sundays ago hoping to get in some practice for races at Berlin dam last weekend. But 'lo, there was no wind. Naturally, wind is as important to sailing as breathing is to humans. "It always happens this way," Commodore Frank Nash of Wadsworth complained. "Every time the press comes around we don't have any wind." "Its good to hear you say that," I replied, "We have the reputation for being pretty windy individuals!"

While we were standing around, pardon the expression, the outboards cut capers on the water while Nash filled me in on the fine art of sailing. "Anyone who can tell you which way the wind is blowing, exclusive of women of course, can be taught to sail in about thirty minutes. However, after the first ten years of it you will be convinced that no one lives long enough to learn it," Nash said. "But what about the women?" I inquired. "How many times has your wife driven the wrong way on a one way street?" he asked. "Oh, I get your point," was my reply.

"What do you do when there is no wind?" my bronzed friend repeated: "Well, beginners are usually bothered by too much wind rather than too little. If there is absolutely no wind at all, we recommend fishing."

"Sailboats in pictures always look like they are about to keel over," I commented. "This is usually done for the benefit of photographers," Nash answered. "Extreme heeling with the decks awash can get a little wet. Sailboats do turn over sometimes; a mishap somewhat more damaging to the ego than anything else."

"Since I wasn't drafted into the Navy your technical terms throw me. Can anyone learn the language?" I asked. "Surprising as it may seem to you, the boats sail just as well without the proper language. However, please learn at least this much about our *Y.*

"It is a low skimmer generally called a lake scow. A scow is not a garbage barge. Some scows, other than the *Y* class, will cost as much as a Cadillac and have more conveniences, including running water. A *Y* is not a rich man's boat although I will admit you can tie quite a bit of money up in one. You can buy them or make them. About 90 percent are constructed on a do-it-yourself plan. A kit would run about $700," Nash explained.

Some quick figuring on the side of the Commodore's sporting trunks indicated that in addition to the kit, $160 worth of Dacron sails, a $125 trailer and other accessories, including swimming lessons at the YMCA, would run the total coat to around $1,200. Anyone who has been around boats very long will confirm a *like new* one can be had for less than half that figure.

Every once in a while the word *fleet* crept into the interview and finally land-lubber ignorance got the best of me, I had to know what a fleet was. Well sir, a *fleet*, according to the *Y-flyer Yacht Racing Association*, is five craft.

The first *Y* fleet was organized at Chippewa Lake. How come? Well, it seems that a chap by the name of Alvin Youngquist of Toledo developed the boat back around 1941. No one seems to know why the craze caught on here. Someone suggested that Parker Beach, Chippewa Lake Park owner, might have met Youngquist somewhere in his travels.

Specifications for an official *Y* fix the length at 18 feet, beam 5 feet-8 inches, weight minimum 500 pounds, sail area 161 feet, and racing crew of two in the United States, and three in Canada.

The words *dry* and *wet* sailing were tossed around rather loosely while we were chatting. I had to know if some new process had been invented to make it possible to sail without water. *Dry* sailing, I learned, is not sailing at all. The terms *dry* or wet indicate whether you take your boat out of water or leave it in between frolics. Boats left in the water will absorb as high as 80-pounds of water, which is the major disadvantage of doing it.

Dacron is now used for sails almost exclusively; considered a high priced man-made fiber it is cheaper than imported English sailcloth that was standard for years and it is practically stretch-proof.

The hour was close to noon so the interview ended. I stepped into my, pardon the expression, outboard and waved a fond farewell to my newfound friends sitting in mournful solitude on the glistening sands. The wind was still in the willow, not on Chippewa Lake.

The Beachcomber

Its funny how close you can work with someone or how well you can get to know him without really getting to know him at all. It never occurred to me to ask what this guy's first job was or how he got interested in the great outdoors. When you are around a chap like Dean "Diz" Sponseller every day you never think to ask what he used to do 'cause this is the kind of a guy you feel you have known all your life.

Diz is one of those likable souls who are typecast for life. He is a tall, lanky outdoor breed who would rather be 30 miles out in the marsh with a rod and reel than about any other place you mention. "If I had all the time in the world and all the money to go with it I would like nothing better than being a beachcomber on a Tahiti sand dune," He will tell you.

One of his favorite pastimes, since he hasn't Tahiti port-of-call money, is to sit quietly with a friend and journey into the land of adventure on the wings of imagination aided and abetted by his keen interest in fishing lore.

Diz also has an interest in offbeat adventure. At one time, he was a professional pallbearer for Cleveland funeral directors who could not round up enough relatives or derelicts to carry bodies to a happy hunting ground.

However, his interest in the great outdoors goes further back than that. "Pop" Sponseller used to take him to quiet streams in the area before our friend was strong enough to hold a pole. By the time he was twelve, he was fly-casting in offbeat haunts of fishermen four times his age.

Getting back to offbeat adventure for the moment, Diz is a wanderer. He shows up where there is excitement. If the excitement is newsworthy, a reporter will pick him out of a crowd guessing he is good copy. Like the time, the spotlight was on Medina and the now-famous Mast-Ammerman murder trial.

Out of the hundreds of local citizens and curiosity seekers who just hung around town while the trial was going on, Diz was one of the people who had his picture big as life in the Columbus Star. His opinion of what was going on was a reporter's idea of the local angle by a *typical* citizen.

As I said, Diz always manages to appear where things are happening as long as they happen outside. The picture in the Star showed him in casual attire resting against an uptown storefront just watching the passing scene. He is the *Marlboro Man* type less the tattoo. He would probably have the tattoo but he did not serve in the Navy during the war. He put his hitch in the infantry.

Becoming an outdoor writer seemed an appropriate ambition for Diz so he tried freelance writing 10 years ago. Naturally it was about fishing and it went to *Outdoor Life* magazine. He got little more than the usual terse rejection slip but not much more; one day the editor did write him a letter to thank him for his effort.

When he did not catch the brass ring for his outdoor tales of the back woods he left town. In 1948, he hired himself out as a guide on the Rifle River in the wilds of upper Michigan. For one whole summer, he drew rations and paltry pay for escorting out-of-town sportsmen into his wonderland of lore. Little did they

23

know that most of the time they knew as much about where they were going as he did.

By the time the summer was over Diz could talk trout with the best of them. He knew every turn in the river from Muskegon to Harbor Springs.

(If some reader who has spent summer vacations on the Rifle notes that it doesn't run between those two popular resort areas and challenges Diz on his geography he will tell them, as he did me, that this only goes to prove he doesn't care what river or stream he is on as long as he has a boat, some grub, and fishing gear.)

Work being unavoidable, Diz labored for the Ohio Fuel Gas Company as a technician back in 1951. Finding his outdoor dreaming somewhat limited by his occupation, he turned to early morning, weekend, and evening escapades at Chippewa Lake. Each year, with the exception of one when he went on a safari to Canada, he returns to his Michigan haunts just for old time's sake. He just got back from a visit to the Au Sable near Lovell.

Some people who are artistically inclined escape to their Shangri-La via the arts. About four years ago Diz whetted his adventure appetite by joining Medina's little theater group better known as the *Masquers*. He has played various roles from a state trooper in *Papa's All* to a mountain boy in *Tobacco Road with Detours*. In the latter, he was magnificent as the hillbilly who lay in the sun, worried about nothing, and had no greater problem in life than how to get a fly off his nose without moving his head.

Diz has studied fishing with the sincerity of a scientist cracking an atom and he knows his business like a master. He can pull big ones out of streams that were *fished out* years ago and he will catch them with casual indifference five feet from where another addict cannot get a nibble.

Knowing the game as he does he will not contribute his good fortune to any set of rules. Old fishing axioms are not worth their weight in bilge water he says.

"You can make a good haul in a downpour or you can pull them in on the hottest dry day of the year. You can make a catch in an east wind and you can do the same if there is not enough breeze to lift a feather. You can get them in Chippewa Lake and you can get them in Thunder Bay. Anywhere you fish, you have to have patience. Even good fishermen lack enough of that," he will tell you.

Yep, that's our boy, that's Dean Sponseller, a patient, soft-spoken young man of 36 who has already caught more fish at home and away than most fishermen get in a lifetime. Diz does not brag about his catches, in fact, you are lucky if you can get you him to tell you how he did on his last trip out. Diz really does not care how many fish he catches or how often. I guess that is the real secret of his success.

Pfundstein's Folly

This is the time of the year when fishermen rummage about the house complaining that the wife has lost their precious fishing tackle, and then go off in a huff to the nearest sporting goods store to get a new supply. If the little woman has not lost the fishing gear, some of it did not hold up too well during winter storage and needs replaced. Our fish starved anglers have a driving urge to look at the latest gimmicks and gadgets. To be very honest about it, any excuse will do.

Even when the snow is up to the eaves our friends of the great outdoors sit by the fire and read *Field and Stream* until they doze off to dream of spring, sunshine and the big one that did not get away. Such a dreamer is Bill Pfundstein of Strongsville, a 31-year employee of the Henry Furnace Company in Medina. A few years ago Bill bought his way into the greatest dream of all, a sure way to catch big bass. He read an ad in one of the popular fishing magazines that guaranteed to show him, for an investment of $15, how to always bring home the limit.

Being a man of modest means but one in search of the fisherman's utopia, Bill sent a money order to Eric Fare of Libertyville, Illinois and received by return mail 24 sheets of instructions and a very ordinary spinning-type lure. The instructions made it immediately clear that the sure-fire guarantee only applied to bass and that if it did not work to return it in 30-days and the 15 bucks would be refunded.

For those of you who have heard of Pfundstein's folly and think you will learn his secret here, it will not be revealed. Bill would not give us the secret at any price. It must remain untold he said, but he did give us some information never before publicly released, as far as we know.

The instructions told him to buy a 15-foot green pole and use it with a one-foot line. "Face into the sun so you will not cast a shadow on the water," it said, and "wear clothes that blend with the background." Finding a green pole was not easy. Bill searched for months and after despair and heartbreak, nearing a point of mental breakdown, he found his pole in a little town called Mt. Idy. Mt. Idy, you may recall, is the place that Charlie Weaver of the Jack Parr show is from.

He then bought a war surplus tent, the old green and gray type, and had it made into a jacket and trousers so he would blend with the landscape. When it came to buying one foot of line, he got into real trouble. He was thrown out of practically every store in Northern Ohio and a couple as far south as Loudenville. He finally bought a full spool and threw away the 99 feet he did not need.

With his son Roy, a Strongsvile High School student, along for moral support Bill headed for East harbor on Lake Erie. To make a long story short, the first try with the secret weapon was of questionable success. Son Roy landed five big bass on worms and Bill got a six-inch bluegill.

That was not the last time our hero took his son along fishing but it was the last time he used the secret weapon where another angler could witness his success. Today Roy goes into hysterics when the subject is mentioned. Bill still insists the secret is foolproof but he has only used it once since that memorable first occasion. This time he went by himself. Again, he made a catch, another six-inch bluegill at Wellington Reservoir.

"I am confident the secret will work but the big drawback is the fact you have to make a darn fool of yourself when you fish. I must look awful silly with the 15-foot green pole and one foot line. You would be surprised how hard it is to find a place to use a one foot line and how much harder it is to get privacy," he said.

"When I answered the ad in the magazine I got back a real sales letter from Fare and also a couple pages of testimonials. They came from all over the country. Its gotta work. Here's what one fella out in Iowa said, 'By golly it works. To be honest with you I had little faith in your ad or even the instructions but I was willing to spend some money to see what you had. After a couple of spots I came to a submerged bush where I had raised a bass several times without being able to handle him. I made a pass only once when all hell broke loose'.

"Another guy said he would sell $150 worth of gear cheap after buying the secret, that in 30-years of fishing he had never seen anything to compare with his results."

Fare claims to have discovered the secret several years ago after spending 18 months in a southern waters search to get a line on the method he had seen used at a little lake in central Illinois by three fisherman who claimed to have picked up the idea down south. He will sell only a limited number of instruction sheets in any given area because; "if it (the secret) becomes known to everybody you and I would no longer have the advantage." He insists that if too many men in a given area already have the secret he will return your money.

Nefarious Fare has graduated from a two-inch ad of two years ago to full-page spreads in national magazines today. If his secret is the art of selling to suckers, he seems to be getting his share of them. Surprisingly enough, Bill does not think he has been a sucker. He still thinks the gimmick will work under the proper conditions.

Where are the lure and instructions now? "Do not tell Florence, that's the little women, but they are in the clothes closet." Bill is going to dig them out from under the umbrella and boots this weekend, and offer them to a friend for 12 bucks. "After all, everyone is going to be fishing electronically soon," he said.

Just last week Bill had a two-way radio installed in his car. "Caught any fish yet?" I asked. "No Mac," was the reply. "So far I only talk to horses. I haven't found the right frequency for fish," Bill said.

Petty Girl Painter

If you have a good memory for important events of World War II you will remember the Japanese-American treaty, which ended the war in the Pacific, was signed on the battleship Missouri in Tokyo Harbor. Franklin Bates of Lodi did not participate in the ceremony but he will always remember the ship as one of the battlewagons for which he laid out camouflage patterns. Bates was a camouflager during the war; in civilian life, he is an artist.

Interest in art for Bates started twenty or thirty years ago. He graduated from Strongsville High School in 1935 and then went on to the Cleveland School of Art. He did his first oil mural for a Strongsville doctor in 1936.

During the war, while he was with the Navy Department on the camouflage assignment, *Lowes State Theater* in Cleveland had an exhibition of his paintings on display. "I guess I was one of the few servicemen who was able to continue my civilian occupation during the war," Bates said.

When military pilots learned that Bates was an artist, he found a lot of his spare time taken up with painting airplane fuselages with *Petty Girl* and other cartoon characters. "The plane crews especially liked the *Playboy* and *Esquire* type art. For a while we got away with giving them about anything they wanted. However, one day The Navy Department decided things were getting out of hand and issued a directive that art should show a little less flesh. "I had to go back over some of my earlier work and add dresses to nearly nude figures," Bates chuckled.

Today he specializes in framed mural landscapes that sell for upwards of $1,000 a piece. The tools he uses to apply the tube-oils to linen canvas are unusual to say the least; a pancake spatula and a palette knife are his only equipment. The oils are squeezed directly from the tube to the canvas and the landscape is then worked out from memory. No brush is ever used.

Because the oils are applied heavily, they create a third dimensional effect that is superior to work with a brush, Bates pointed out. It takes 25 tubes of studio size color at $8 a tube for the average size mural.

Although his studios are in Lodi Bates spends most of his time *on the job* all over Medina, Wayne and Summit counties. "Wall murals are becoming increasingly popular today and you can't bring that kind of art into a studio," he said. Doctor Andrew Karson of Medina has two of Bates' murals in his office and Charles Sheets has a Lake Louise scene on one wall of his Ryan Road home. Three of Bates' works are on loan to the Bunker Hill Restaurant north of Medina where they are on display in a new smorgasbord room. The Merle Auker residence on CR141 south of Brunswick displays a Bates' painting valued at over $500.

Bates has little use for so-called modern art. In his opinion, modern artists are those who lack ability or talent to paint what they and the buying public see so they use the modern art theme since no one can say their impressions are, or are not, accurate.

The 43-year old artist went modern only on one occasion and that was about twenty years ahead of the times. In 1935, he painted his automobile two-tone lavender and red. He also did quite a bit of pin-stripping which has become the rage of late among the hotrod crowd.

"Art popularity like anything else runs in cycles," Bates explained. The *Gibson* and *Petty Girl* art of the past two wars is not nearly so popular as landscapes. That will change and one of these days calendars and magazines will be back. The only difference will be some new artist will be doing the work and making the money from *new found* art," he concluded.

2005 Update: In 1933 *Esquire* magazine was born. It featured the origin of the American pin-up, *The Petty Girl* by George Petty. The magazine became an instant newsstand hit. The airbrush art of Petty was so popular he also sold it to *Jantzen* swimsuits, *Old Gold Cigarettes*, *Pepsi Cola* and many other advertisers. The hood ornament of the 1951-54 Nash automobile was a Petty design. In 1950 the movie *Petty Girl* starred Joan Caufield and Robert Cummings. *Petty Girl* art was every where.

Esquire replaced Petty with Peruvian artist Alberto Vargas in the 1940s and the *Varga Girl* was born for $75 a week. Vargas later went to work for *Playboy* and stayed there for 18 years. He is perhaps better remembered than Petty but it was Petty and his airbrush art that started the pin-up craze of the 1930s, '40s and '50s.

Ace Brigode and the Birth of Radio

Ace Brigode gave up his real name a long time ago because, as he tells it, in those days you didn't keep a name frowned on by the Church and Athos was in that class. Ace's dad tagged him with the name Athos because he liked the swashbuckling dash of *The Three Musketeers* as described in Alexander Dumas's famous book. Athos, you may recall, was one of the three musketeer characters.

Maybe Athos Brigode would have stayed in the profession of making window glass, inherited from his father and traditionally picked up by the son of he family, but Ace had too much dash. Until 12 years ago grass never grew under his feet. Although his formal training as a musician started when he was nine years old, Ace never credited his talent for the success of his bands, which climbed to the top during the roaring 20's.

Like all fledging young musicians, Ace read *Billboard* and hoped for the day when his name would be emblazoned across page one. He wasn't sure how to accomplish the dream but when he saw a classified ad by the *Brown-Roberts Virginia Dramatic Company,* he figured he was on the right road if they would hire him. He played the clarinet and had made a cross-country trip with the *Toledo Newsboy's Band.* They did hire him, somewhat to his surprise, and found he was not only a good musician but he had a talent for acting.

His road show acting career, with a little music thrown in, was cut short by World War I. He went back to his father's glass factory. When the war ended, Ace got back into the theater by forming his own dramatic company, and immediately losing his shirt. By this time he was only 23 years old but in road-show circles his name was so well known that the famous Al. G. Fields, of *Field's Minstrels*, drafted him and his saxophone sextet. A year later the Army drafted him. He just could not get started.

After some bouncing around in the Navy, he landed in Charleston, West Virginia where a gun plant hiring 2000 civilians, and billeting enough military brass to win a war single handedly, was in dire need of entertainment. Ace formed a band. When his services were not required at the plant he and his musicians would make one night stands in Charleston and at other coal mining towns in the area. One night stands were unheard of in those days.

The only traveling shows were circuses and dramatic companies. Since this was before the era of the automobile, travel was by train. Ace and his band would catch a mainline train and get off on a spur going back into the hills. There they would hop on a handcar and work their way back to a mineshaft community where they would entertain until early morning and then take the handcar back to the mainline where they would flag the next train back to Charleston.

Overnight the huge gun plant was closed and one-niters became Ace's bread and butter, at $40 a night for nine musicians, he couldn't afford much else. To give his hungry band prestige, he named them the *Virginians* and used *"Carry Me Back to Old Virginia"* as his theme song. There were no agencies in those days to find work for entertainers, they found their own. Up to this time, there wasn't much work to be had. Since road bands were unheard of, club proprietors were tough to sell on the idea of hiring a band for a night or two. From Rock Island, Illinois to Charleston, West Virginia seems like the wrong way to Broadway but Ace got there; he made it when the country was going mad.

His first break came when he signed a 30 day contract for a stint at Philadelphia's famous Walton Hotel rooftop nightclub, and stayed for eleven months. That was 1922. The East was just starting to taste jazz and under-the-table-liquor. Prohibition was in and the lid was off. The country was going crazy in so many ways that, according to Ace, the *Roaring Twenties* was far crazier than writers have been able to portray. The government was making half-hearted attempts to bring some sanity to the era and Ace lost his first job because of it. General Smedley Butler of the Quantico Marines was sent to Philadelphia to clean things up. Marines were posted at nightspots around the city and at the rooftop elevator to the dance floor where the *Virginians* were playing. Each arrival was searched before he or she was allowed to take a table. If they had a flask it was taken away and sometimes, they were too. With this kind of shakedown going on customers soon decided, it was less risky to stay home and drink bathtub gin. Butler didn't clean up Philadelphia. He finally gave up, saying politics made it impossible to dry up the city. In the meantime, Ace decided to shoot the works and crash New York.

He opened at the Monte Carlo, which was the sportsmen's rendezvous of the day. Ace has a picture in his office at Chippewa

Lake showing the band, entertainers and guests who attended a testimonial dinner for Jack Dempsey after his defeat of Georges Carpentier at *Boyle's Thirty Acres* in Jersey City in 1921. He could not have picked a better spot. The post-war decade was a great sports era. Remember Jones of golf, Tilton of tennis, Grange and Rockne of football, the Four Horsemen, and many, many other greats of the era?

Radio was about to change the habits of the American public then, just as television has changed our era. The first broadcast was made from *KDKA Pittsburgh* in 1920. However, few people showed any interest in wireless telephony but just about the time Ace hit Broadway, everyone was talking about it. You couldn't buy a radio but you could put together circuits, detectors, neutrodynes and sodion tubes, and come up with a gadget capable of picking sounds out of the air. Ace made make his first broadcast from McKeesport, Pennsylvania, which also had a *KDKA* station.

Meanwhile, back in New York *Radio Station WJZ*, owned by *RCA's* Davis Sarnoff, was getting into the act. Sarnoff offered Ace a chunk of RCA stock for $38 a share but he scoffed at the price. By 1929, it was worth $549 a share! Sarnoff wanted to try broadcasting from the Monte Carlo so he and his crew, which outnumbered the *Virginians*, set up shop there. Every musician had a mike. It was a big operation. The orchestra was also making once a week broadcasts from station *WNYZ* that was in City Hall 10 miles from the Monte Carlo. After finishing their floorshow at the Monte Carlo, a waiting black Mariah, with a motorcycle escort, would race through the streets to arrive in time for a broadcast there. One time Al Jolson made the wild trip with Ace and said if he had to do that to make a living he would give up singing. "We were scared stiff every week but Police Commissioner Grover Whalen wanted us to do it so we did," Brigode said.

It was a crazy, crazy era. So much happened to Ace in such a short period there just isn't time enough, or space enough, to write it all down. For example, the Virginians were in a movie made on Long Island called *Haunted Hands*. The band was recording for five companies, *Columbia, OK (Okee), Harmony* and two others. Their big recording *Yes Sir, That's My Baby* sold around 800,000 records and was the smash hit in the country at the time.

"Our band was enjoying tremendous popularity and I think a great deal of it was due to the arrangements of Frank Skinner. At the time there was only one other band that used arrangements," he explained. In addition to Skinner, great artists like Abe Lincoln on the trombone and Tommy Thompson on the drums played with the band. Thompson, a Medina boy, graduated from Julliard, and is now the head percussionist for the *Boston Symphony Orchestra*.

Ace had many friends in the entertainment world. One of the best was Fats Waller. Skitch Henderson of the Steve Allen television show is another. Steve will mention Ace every once in a while on his show. Early in Ace's career a couple of boys, Jimmy and Tommy, from Lanceford, Pennsylvania would sit in with his group when it played at Tomokway. They were the Dorsey Brothers.

Ace said he was one of the first band leaders to take his musicians on the road. He bought an old *Fageol* that was as contrary as a coal mine mule. In 1927 Brigode's New York band came to Cleveland's *Danceland*. Tom Manning was his announcer for a weekly WTAM radio broadcast. While there, a stint at Youngstown *Idora Park* broke all attendance records.

Then in 1930 Ace and his band went to Chicago to play at *Merry Gardens* where they stayed for eleven years. There he had a radio broadcast called the *Blue Hour*. It drew such response from 1AM to 2PM that the time slot also attracted many commercials. Before that time, station management assumed everyone was in bed by midnight.

During another summer tour Ace played at the 1936 *Dallas, Texas Fair* and set an all-time attendance record there of 57,000 people in one day. Ace says the secret of that success was the fact it was a blistering hot day and the ballroom was air-conditioned. Elliott Roosevelt, who owned the *Texas Radio Network*, asked Brigode to broadcast from Chippewa Lake[1] the following year. It took seven miles of special wire from there to main transmission lines. The wire is still there today and so is Brigode. He broke up his band in 1946 and came to Chippewa Lake to stay in 1948 where he has handled promotions, publicity and public relations ever since. This year he is celebrating his tenth year of retirement. He would like to write a book about his experiences but the kind of retirement that Ace settled for doesn't leave him time to write. We hope he finds time soon. His story is the kind that should be preserved.

2005 Update: Ace never wrote his book, he died February 3, 1960. He probably should be a legend, but historians have written little about his adventurous life.

---

[1] The Park opened in 1878 and closed 100 years later. On June13, 2002 a fire burned most of what remained.

In fact, you will have a difficult time finding any music publications that even mention his name. He is referred to on many computer web sites but most of them only say, "He was dance band leader," none contain the detail of my 1950s interview with him.

A few of the web sites elaborate on details of his life that he had not revealed in my interview with him, but I have not authenticated their accuracy. One said, in addition to my reference to his hit record *Yes Sir. That's My Baby*, he had several others including *Wait 'Til Its Moonlight*, *Alabamy Bound* and *Goin' Home*[2]. It noted that a radio program of his was called *The White Rose Gasoline Show*. One said he played the violin; he had only referred to the clarinet in my interview.

This Internet site also said it was rumored that former President Dwight Eisenhower, upon hearing of Ace's death, played a 78-rpm record of Brigode's *Sleeping Beauty Wedding* as he sat alone in the Oval Office.[3]

My search for current information on Ace led me to seeking his sheet and recorded music. I found records of the sheet music, none of which are available to buy, and only one remastered track of one of his songs on an audio compact disc album.

The Title of the album is *The Charleston Era* [AJA 5342] by AJA London, England first sold in 2000 and is still available. The album contains 25 sound tracks of some still remembered famous, and now unknown, musical entertainers. A few of the names you

---

[2] There were probably more
[3] I have been unable to confirm any of these details from known sources.

may recall are Fred Astaire, Bing Crosby, Duke Ellington, Paul Whiteman, Fred Waring, George Gershwin, Al Jolson, Victor Young, and Ace Brigode. The original tracts were recorded between March 1925 and October 1930. Brigode's tract is "Yes Sir, That's My Baby!" Made in New York, April 30,1925.

Peter Dempsey, one of two men credited with putting the album collection together from the original 78rpm records-the other was Ray Crick- defines the *Charleston Era* as beginning about 1925. He notes, "its first real emergence came at the *Jungles Casino* in Charleston, Carolina in 1913, and it was therefore already well established in the popular Negro American vocabulary."

As I reread my original story about Ace I was struck by the coincidence that his jazz band career started in Charleston, West Virginia not Charleston, South Carolina. On the other hand, since the *Charleston Era* took the whole world by storm, it should be no surprise that West Virginia was also caught up in the Ragtime whirlwind.

Dick Booth

"I don't think there will be a World War IV," he said. "You mean World War III," I replied, correcting his error. "No, I mean World War IV. If we have another war it will be the last one but I don't think we will have another conflict, at least I hope not."

It was last Saturday morning. I had dropped in to see Dick Booth who has been around these parts for 80 years. Booth isn't a student of national or international affairs nor does he have much respect for politics, but I figured anyone who has been around since 1877 must have some knowledge and observations that we youngsters can't back up with personal experience.

RB, who at 80 still puts in an active 10-hour day, six and seven days a week work schedule, is physically and mentally 20 years younger than the record shows. Because he is keenly interested in what makes this democracy of ours tick, we got a particular kick out of talking to him.

Booth is a carpenter. He was born in Vermont and then made his way to Chicago where he practiced his trade for 17 years. He became a foreman for the McKeown Brothers of the Windy City and was involved in what must have been one of the contracting forerunners of today's prefabricated buildings. The McKeowns had seen wood truss roofs constructed in Belfast, Ireland. They brought the idea to America just as the demand for garages to house new gas buggies was being heard. The truss-roofed buildings were wanted from the Dakotas to New York and the McKeowns did their best to supply the demand. RB was in charge of traveling state to state and city to city building the hanger-like structures.

According to Booth, in those days automobile garages were built for the purpose of housing cars not repairing them as it is today. "Few people had private places to keep their buggies in those days so centrally located garages were built. It was not until keeping the gas buggy going became a specialized business that the garages had any other use."

On one of his trips east, Booth had some work to do in Cleveland. When that was done he returned to Chicago but a carpenter strike was on so he decided it was about time to settle down. His local supervisor bought a farm in Medina County and he came down to help him run it; that was 1920.

RB did a variety of farm and carpentry work for the next ten years including the construction of the Medina Machine Shop at 113 East Smith Road. Then the depression came along and everything seemed to stop except the necessity of eating. He knew farmers were still eating so he decided to get into a business that would rely on farmers for income so his forging, welding and repair business came into being; he has been at that trade ever since.

Although Booth has no particular interest in politics he knows more about the subject than most of us and he has some observations to make. If we assume that he thinks what most of us will think about the world in general after we experience its ups and down for 80 years, then his comments should be interesting.

"I have watched the slow evolution of our country to what we call a democracy. With all the fears and reservations that statesmen have I think the social and industrial progress of our country makes it evident that so-called socialization of our economy has not been in error. I don't want anybody to accuse me of being a radical but I think our high standard of living can be attributed, in part, to liberal government modified to meet the demands of the public.

"I don't share with some folks the idea that we should hate Communists. The people are entitled to their own opinion as to what is best for them. After all, democracy as we once knew it has been modified considerably. What is democracy today would have been radical thinking just 20 years ago. People have a right to their own form of government regardless of what label you put on it."

Speaking of politicians, RB said the first president he voted for was William Jennings Bryan. I voted for every candidate of the Democratic Party until Eisenhower came along, then I switched. "Not that I thought there was anything wrong with the Democrats but because I thought, for the first time in my life, they had nothing to offer in the way of a potential president; under the circumstances Ike was a better choice."

"What one invention do you think has had the biggest impact on America, you have seen almost every one of them. Which do you think made the biggest change in our way of life?" I asked. "That question is easy to answer. Anyone will tell you that the coming of the automobile changed life in these United States like no invention before or since." "Aside from the auto what other invention has most impressed you? Was it television perhaps?"

"No, television didn't seem to me to be particularly astounding but the coming of the old 5-cent silent movie and the radio did. I can't remember anything that used to thrill me like those old movies. I played around with radio. It was an expensive hobby at first. Back in those days, as I recall, it took about $100 to build a receiving set, tubes cost $7.50 a piece and I couldn't afford speakers so earphones were standard equipment."

"Has Medina changed much as you remember it?" I asked. "I suppose it has but when you grow up with the changes they don't seem to be impressive. Of course when I first came here there were very few paved roads. The best way to get to Cleveland from Medina was to drive to Brunswick, from there to Hinckley, and then up State Road to Lake City. We didn't like to drive North of Brunswick because an old stone road there was really rough."

Has Booth's business changed much since the encroachment of the city on rural farms? You bet it has. For example, last year he repaired somewhere around 500 plow points, he had done at least twice that many in previous seasons. "A new throw-away *Radex* Blade-type point has made a big difference too. The throwaway point was at first patented by *Oliver* but it is now on a number of tractors. They only cost between two and three dollars depending on the size. It costs that much to repair the other type. The other ones have to have new blades and points welded in my shop then pounded out on my forge. The new ones are just bolted on. I think the new blade is as good as the old type but some of the old-timers are not convinced yet. On their old equipment, they still have to use old type blades. One of these days they will be using the new ones because I think all of the new equipment will come with that type."

Booth is now doing more truck work than ever because of the decline in the farm business. He is busier than most men of 65 and will continue to work hard until someone makes him quit. He attributed his good physical and mental condition to heredity rather than diet or living habits. Both his mother and father lived to 80 years of age and his grandparents exceeded the 90 mark. He thinks drinking to excess is ridiculous but does not see anything morally or physically wrong with moderation. "If we used moderation in everything we do, all of us would have less problems economically, socially, physically and politically," Booth concluded.

Blaze In

I will tell you right now, if I knew what I was getting into Monday, I would not have taken the assignment that produced this story!

It all began Thursday morning when the boss said they were going to 'blaze in' an oil well down Chatham way and I should go down there for the occasion. It just so happened they did not 'blaze in' the well that day and I was happy about the whole thing because I never liked to work the day before a holiday.

Monday morning a bright young fellow by the name of Dave Bolton came bounding into the office, "Well, are you ready to go?" Since I had only been in for about an hour and it was the first time I had been there in four days, I thought it was a little early to be going anywhere, besides, I didn't know to where he was taking me. Dave said he had run into my boss someplace over the weekend and he was supposed to tell me that I was to go to Chatham come Monday am.

As I said before, I had not been in the office for four days. I was behind in my work but who am I to argue with the top banana. We were off to Chatham. As we bounced along West Smith Road-Dave's car rides like the pouch of a kangaroo-I just couldn't understand what I was doing heading for the wilds on a day when Chatham was about as interesting as the belly of a muskrat, a wet muskrat. It was raining.

About 15 minutes and six million bounces later we were sitting in the office of Paul Baldwin, president of *Baldwin Producing Corporation*. Baldwin was already explaining to *Cleveland Plain Dealer* reporter Sam Marshall that the well he was going to bring in was 385 feet deep and his driller, Forrest Lovett of Lodi, told him it was the best one he had seen in his 35 years in the oil fields.

About this time, a worker came in to tell us we were welcome out at the well. We donned slickers, boots, and steel helmets and headed for the bush. I wasn't sure what the helmet was for but I figured it had been furnished more for appearance sake than necessity. We drove back a muddy, axle deep road, twisted and turned through a jungle-like woods and finally stopped in a clearing 10 feet from a dank, murky swamp. There, high and dry, was a picturesque rig towering over a picturesque shack near a picturesque truck labeled explosive...explosive! A chap dressed in blue denims was fussing around with a winch on the back of the truck when we arrived. He was introduced as C. M. Richardson, oil and gas well shooter of Lodi.

"Now if you gentlemen will step right over here," Richardson said as he motioned to our party, "I will let you watch us pour the fifth shell full of nitro-glycerin...WATCH US POUR THE FIFTH SHOT OF NITRO-GLYCERIN! Sam, Dave, an insurance salesman, and I all backed off about ten paces and smiled persimmon-sucking smiles...NITRO-GLYCERIN? "You can stand back there if you want to but if something goes wrong, whether you are there or here, there won't be enough pieces to pick up."

My mind flashed back to a picture Baldwin had shown us in his office of the remains of a horse, wagon, and man. When something set off a load of nitro, there was not enough left to photograph. Whomever took the picture penned a note along the side of it which said, "Sorry this is all there was." I also remember reading somewhere that dynamite was invented because nitro was too dangerous to handle.

Dynamite is sawdust soaked with nitro to protect it from shock. What was I doing here watching them pour the last of 116 quarts of the stuff into a shell that would be lowered gently into the well? Very gently. I walked back and leaned on a fender of the truck as Richardson explained that the blast would be aimed away from the rig by an angled piece of welded pipe fitted on top of the well after the last shell had been lowered. Baldwin then told us to notice how gingerly Richardson handled the empty container as he walked to the truck with it. "Empty cans have been known to blow up, truck and all," he said.

After the last shell was lowered into the well and a wire was strung to a plunger 100 feet away, we were told to move to the edge of the swamp, except for Richardson who was waiting to push the plunger.

A downward thrust-we waited-nothing happened. "Guess we got a short," he said as he went back to the wellhead to disconnect the wire. His two helpers produced new wire and we again waited. Down went the plunger again-nothing happened.

Baldwin jumped into a jeep and pulled it up to where the plunger was located. "We'll use the battery to set off the charge," he said as he lifted the hood. Richardson walked over to the vehicle, hollered *ready* and touched the wire to the battery. There was a pause, the ground rocked and then with a roar oil, water and Berea limestone shot 200 feet in the air, made a gentle arch, and fell back to mother earth.

When it appeared the big blow was over a second geyser, much higher than the first, rose into the sky with another roar. "Look at that color! Look at that oil!" Baldwin shouted with the glee of a three-year-old kid seeing his first giraffe. The nito had been used to break the rock strata and allow the oil to run into the well.

The strike may always be remember by Paul Baldwin and his associates as the biggest in the history of their firm. I will remember it as the most dangerous assignment I ever had in this business of news reporting.

Busy Sky

Highways of Medina County are crowded. Few people realize that the skyways over our heads are confronted with the same problem. We have been hearing about it during the past few weeks after several air accidents focused national attention on the situation.

How many aircraft do you suppose fly over Medina County in 24-hours? The experts do not like to guess, but the CAA (Civil Aeronautics Authority)[4] told this reporter Saturday, "In 24 hours controlled aircraft would average around 1000." He then hastened to add, "The 1000 figure is only a drop in the bucket because there is a lot of traffic up there we know nothing about."

What is controlled aircraft? Frankly, it is tough to explain in laymen's language. If pilots will forgive me I'll simplify it by saying if you want the FAA on the ground to keep track of your flight in the air you may file a flight plan with a traffic control center. The center will follow the flight on paper by keeping a record of the speed and altitude information you give them. They will see to it that you are properly spaced in time and altitude away from other aircraft.

If the CAA is watching the progress of the aircraft why all the fuss about air safety and why have there been collisions and near

---

[4] Renamed the Federal Aviation Authority (FAA) in 1958

misses? You will note we have been talking about controlled aircraft. There are not any regulations that require pilots to use the CAA control facilities. The CAA can only give the relationship in the air of one controlled aircraft to another controlled aircraft. A military, civilian or commercial aircraft that gets in the path of a controlled flight cannot be anticipated. Where aircraft are under CAA control accidents and near misses between them are rare indeed.

Getting back to the matter of airspace, you may incorrectly guess that there is plenty of room in the sky for everyone. The correct answer to that can be likened to the situation on the ground. On back roads, traffic is generally light. Even if you drove carelessly, the odds of running into anyone would be rare. On main roads leading into big cities, you would get into trouble quickly. Take Route 42 into Cleveland for example, it is a very dangerous highway to travel under any circumstances because traffic is heavy. The same is true in the air. Around big cities, traffic is intense.

Highways in the sky are laid out in much the same fashion as they are on the ground; they converge on big cities. Over Medina the skyways lead into and out of Cleveland including Routes V-30, R-20, A-6, V-40, V-42, V-75, V-103 and R-19. Routes V-30, V-75, V-40 and R-19 pass directly over Medina. Routes V-42 and R-20 pass directly over Brunswick. When unidentified aircraft wonder in and around these routes, there is a chance an air collision might occur.

We mentioned earlier that there are not any rules that require pilots to use control facilities. You might assume that the quick solution to the problem would be to direct them to do so.

Highways on the ground and those in the air are not keeping up with the times. There are not enough controllers or equipment to handle all of the traffic.

Like our traffic regulations on the ground, there are traffic regulations for the sky. If pilots fly on or cross highways in the sky there are certain rules which govern their actions. For example, if visibility is less than three miles they are required to file a flight plan with the CAA. If they do not fly near the airways and fly at altitudes more than 3000 feet they must fly at specified heights for given directions of flight. In other words, this is similar to the requirement on the ground that you drive on the right side of the road to avoid collisions. Pilots flying within given distances of airports must maintain certain heights and approach particular runways as specified by written regulations for small airports and specific radio instructions at larger ones.

Fatal accidents do not happen as often in the air as on the ground. The passenger fatality rate for commercial airlines is .89 per 100 million miles. During 1957, the rate was 5.9 for the same amount of miles in passenger cars.

When weather conditions are CAVU (ceiling and visibility unlimited) CAA control centers are not over-taxed. During the time that conditions are bad controllers work to the limit of their physical and mental capabilities because more aircraft are using their services. CAA officials will confirm that most air collisions and near misses, however are in good weather. Again, like the situation on the ground, when the weather is bad everyone is more cautious.

It appears obvious that everyone using or crossing aerial skyways in any kind of weather should be required to file flight plans with a CAA control center. As so often is the case, unless and until more trained personnel and equipment are available we must make the most of what we have. Under present circumstances, the CAA appears to be doing a magnificent job.

Wall Street Mink

George Siedel, owner of the mink ranch just north of Medina on Route 42, will be watching the stock market closely from now until June. Siedel is not a broker and does not have an interest in Wall Street but he knows a healthy market is a good sign that the price of mink pelts will also be good. The opposite is true if the market nose-dives.

Reading the *Wall Street Journal* is one of the more pleasant aspects of being a mink rancher. While the operation is scientific from beginning to end, a lot of hard work has to be plowed into the business to make it a worthwhile enterprise. Back in 1940, the average rancher was losing $1.04 on every mink he marketed. It does not take an accountant to prove you do not survive long with such a state of affairs existing. Today, the mink business is doing all right for itself but there is always a big element of chance to contend with.

Before the mink era, fox ranchers were riding high. If you did not have a fox fur coat or a tail or two thrown over your shoulder you were from the wrong side of the tracks. Now fox farms are as rare as horse-drawn carriages and apparently the big reason for the decline can be attributed to women's privilege of changing her mind; today she prefers mink.

Siedel started his Strongsville mink raising business in 1933. Just before World WarII, he purchased the present land site for further expansion but the war canceled out everything. Like most of the country's other ranchers, George sold his mink and started to carry a rifle. By 1946, the ranchers were back home starting all over again from scratch. That year 291,000 mink were marketed compared with last year's total of over 4,000,000.

The pelts are air expressed to New York City where, for a 5 percent commission, fur brokers handle grading, bundling, showing and the sale of the furs. The sales are conducted January through June with the exception of March when the ranchers are too busy breeding mink to be bothered by the financial details.

The mink rancher advises his broker when to sell and at what price. If prices appear to be about at their peak, Siedel will sell early in the season. If the best guessers in the business predict higher prices later, and he agrees with them, he may hold all or parts of his pelts until the prices move up. The trick of the trade is to know when to sell. "Last month we shipped 5,700 pelts to the market and the way things look they should bring a pretty good price this year," Siedel explained.

"We still have about 2,100 females and 400 males for breeding purposes," he continued. "Incidentally, the biggest price I ever paid for a breeder was $1,200 for a sapphire back in 1948. At that time there was only 1,800 of them in the country. Since 1942, American breeders have developed a number of what we call color mutations including platinum, pastel, iris, pearl, purple-glow and palomino. There are many other varieties and all were developed from the original dark natural color brown."

Siedel's 28 year old ranch manager Jerry Hoffman probably knows more about mink than anyone in the country of his same age. He started in the business when he was eleven years old and has been at it ever since. He knows everything about the operation from the care and feeding of kits, as the young are called, to the different analysis of fur pelt quality.

Mink are pelted once a year in December. The operation includes killing, skinning, freezing, and fleshing. The process of fleshing is the final dressing up of the skin, removing excess fat by scraping.

"It takes 60 to 70 mink, half male and half female, to make an average size coat. While the width of each pelt is only about four inches, skilled craftsmen, earning as high as $5 an hour slit each hide at half-inch intervals. They are thus able to spread the pelt and resew it so perfectly that not only is the size increased but the beauty of the fur is improved," Huffman said.

"Mink are hungry creatures," he explained as he moved from pen to pen looking after his charges. "Ours consume 2 to 2 1/2 tons a day of fish, liver, cereal, cottage cheese, buttermilk, yeast and tomato pulp. You must keep them well fed if you want them to produce an acceptable fur. Proper diet is most important and is carefully controlled. If human diet was as closely watched as that of our mink doctors would have less cause for concern and the American public would save millions of dollars each year."

Baby Ace

In this age of Sputniks, guided missiles and hydrogen bombs, we are apt to forget the aviation pioneers who made getting away from earth a personal responsibility. This is not true of all of us as any EAA member can confirm. EAA stands for Experimental Air Association, which is a national organization that promotes the back shop activities of air enthusiasts.

Junior Armbruster, who operates a 77-acre farm 6½ miles south of Medina, is an EAA member. He has just completed building a flyable airplane that was started in 1955. This week CAA officials will look over Armbruster's *Baby Ace* and give it the government's blessing or instruct it's builder to make changes so that the miniature plane will pass rigid airworthy tests.

Chances are the CAA will stamp an OK on Junior's project because the 34-year old mechanic-farmer is meticulously particular about how the plane is put together and has already gotten CAA approval of the craft's structural skeleton. The pocket size plane is only 17 feet long and has a wingspan of 25 feet. The engine is a 65 hp *Lycoming*, the same power plant used in the popular "Cub."

The *Baby Ace* plans appeared in Mechanic's Illustrated magazine three years ago and Armbruster decided he would try his hand at putting together the pint-size sport plane that was conceived in 1930. The plane never went into mass production because most of the aircraft built in those days were put together as part time hobbies of youngsters who envisioned a bright future for aviation but had little more than talent and junk parts to work with. People with money just would not invest in such bad risk enterprises.

The only parts in the *Baby Ace* that were not made on the farm with loving care are the engine, landing gear and the instruments. Even the spruce spars and ribs were cut out of bigger timbers in Armbruster's cowshed workshop. Aircraft steel tubing was painstakingly welded together for the fuselage. The wings and body are covered with fabric, which has been painted Caribbean blue and white.

The one passenger craft was issued an identification number N5775 after the CAA structural inspection but Armbruster cannot flight test the plane until an experimental certificate is issued. When flight approval is received, it may only be flown within 25 miles of the farm during the first 25 hours of engine time. The CAA will then approve clearance to fly more extensive missions.

Flying is not new to Armbruster although this is his first effort to build his own plane. He took lessons in 1946 while helping his father run an implement business in the city. He credits his mechanical abilities in part to his farm tractor experience.

Armsbruster expects the small 598 pound plane to have a flight radius of about 300 miles and hopes that the CAA will authorize him to make a cross-country flight to the annual EAA convention in Milwaukee early in August.

Eddie Paul

Eddie Paul is the son of a baker. "Pop" Paul brought his family to Medina around 1925 and opened the Medina Bakery, which was located in a building that is now the side of Null's diner on North Court Street. Eddie worked in the bakery while attending high school. He earned spending money but like most young fellows did not have much left for investment after buying soda pop and candy at the corner drugstore.

Most folks can remember some individual, incident, or ambition that urged them to start in the profession that they chose, but the circumstances are a total blank in Eddy's case. He does remember that he had a burning desire to play the accordion and Charles Magnante was his idol. While the details of what brought about this interest are vague, Eddie remembers the contract he negotiated with his father in order to buy an accordion and learn how to play it.

"Somehow we came to terms of a salary of eight dollars per week for services rendered at the bakery. In those days eight bucks was not big money but I did not think it was bad until I started figuring my expenses. Five dollars each week went toward the purchase of the accordion. It cost me a dollar to get to Cleveland and back on the bus for lessons and they were $1.50 each. So I had 50-cents left over to throw around! About three months and twelve lessons later, I was invited to Granger to do a single with Paul Brando's orchestra that was playing for a banquet at the school. To give me a buildup I was listed as out of Cleveland.

"Well, it came time for my number and I started my first selection. Before I got to the chorus the room became quiet and I could sense the guests were listening. It was not talent that made them spellbound, believe me. The reason was a piano-accordion was a new sound. I am not sure, but I think that I had one of the first such instruments in the area and my audience was attracted by the novelty.

"To make a long story short, I was riding high until I finished two numbers and then came back for an encore. Brando called me over after the third number and said, 'Boy, you've get them eating out of your hand, go out there and give them some more'. Some more! There wasn't any more! I had learned only three pieces! Soon after that, I formed my own band. I took my new nine pieces into Fixler's Ballroom at Wadsworth. Our big attraction then was a gal booked as Shari, a blues singer."

There were local boys playing Paul's *That Rhythm You Can't Resist* including Ev. England, Gaylord Smith, and Jerry Broomall on saxs, Eugene Beck on trumpet, Harold Spahr on violin, Austin Vanna at the piano, Charles Ewing at the base and George Sponseller on the drums. The band played for a number of occasions around the area including sorority and frat sessions at B.W.

By 1936 our three-song artist had picked up additional tunes and was booked in at the Columbia ballroom on Route 82. He was so pleased with himself he walked into the side of a truck while dreaming up new arrangements. However, music is relaxing and our most happy fella came out of the fray with swathes of bandages and only minor injuries. The records show Eddie played 26 consecutive weeks at Columbia. This fact does not mean much to a layman but it meant bread and butter for the combo. Like fighters who have consecutive wins, the same accomplishment at a ballroom means you are a good draw and worth a nice piece of change to management.

Billboard Magazine was keeping track of Paul and his gang. They reported in their May 14, 1948 issue that he had opened at Elberta Beach. *Consolidated Radio Artists*, booking out of offices in New York City, picked up Paul and his group to fill engagements around the state. A number of fine orchestras were in the CRA stable, including an up and coming fellow by the name of Paul Whiteman. Mentor, Summit Beach Park, Akron's East Market Gardens, Edgewater Park, and Columbia were part of the Eddie Paul circuit. Radio station WGAR along about this time started to feature Paul's band on a direct pickup from the Columbia ballroom three nights a week.

In 1939, a publishing firm by the name of Evan Georgeoff published the band's theme song *Stolen Moments*. Wendell Given, an Orville boy and the band's arranger, wrote the music.

Then came the war and Uncle Sam began to whittle away at the Eddie Paul contingent until he finally threw in the sponge and joined the *Seabees*. Stationed in England as a cook, Paul lost no time in organizing a Yankee dance orchestra and immediately joined the base military band. "We had a great time playing in England but I never worked under such adverse conditions," Paul said. "I had to be up at 3 AM to prepare breakfast for the boys.

We would play downtown and get in at midnight. Three hours of sleep at best would hardly be enough and to top it off, just as sure as we would hit the sack, air raid sirens would scream and a nights sleep would end before I had a chance to close my eyes."

Medina, New York

Occasionally the City of Medina, NY comes up in local conversation. The obvious similarity between that city and our own is, of course, the name. A quick look at the map will disclose several other comparative factors. Communities are about 30 miles from the Great Lakes, both are close to Akron, Ohio and both have about the same size population. Recently each city completed a successful hospital fund-raising drive. It was coincidence that they were planned for the same time. It did aroused speculation as to whether we had other things in common. To get the answer I drove to Medina, NY last weekend.

The comparisons found are so surprising you may wonder, as I did, if somewhere back in our early history someone from that area was around to suggest the name for our town when it was chosen. Local historical records do not prove or disprove the possibility.

As you drive into the New York community from the west, the land is flat just as here. Entering the downtown area on State Highway 31, you pass the railroad station, cross the tracks and there is Medina. In downtown general appearance, there is no likeness; the town is not built around a square. While this lack of sameness discourages a perfect comparison picture, there are many other likenesses. As I drove around one of the first buildings that caused a double take was the postoffice. The same reaction was my response to seeing the school.

Medina, NY has a small commercial airport, diversified small industry and beautiful old residential sections. There are a smattering of new homes and new streets. We share exactly the same number of churches, we have four drugstores to their three, each has three jewelers, two ten-cents stores and three cleaning establishments. All other retail field comparisons are close, very close.

In the food processing industry, both cities have pickle factories; New York has *H. J. Heinz* and we have *H. W. Madison.* Other small businesses there include *General Foods Birds Eye* plant, *American Brake Shoe Company, Casting Division* (a completely automatic operation), the *California Spray Chemical Company, White Brothers Rose Corporation*, one of the largest growers of indoor roses east of the Mississippi, *R. H. Newell Company*, manufacturers of custom shirts and pajamas, *Hickey-Freeman Clothiers, A. L. Swett Iron Works*, and many others.

Each of our communities has just completed school building projects. A new centralized elementary school dedicated in Medina NY in 1956 provides educational facilities for over 1,200 area students. The necessity of the school was brought about by consolidation of the Medina school system with 24 rural school districts. The word consolidation is not a new one here in Ohio and our school building program is comparable in financial costs.

This quote from their Chamber of Commerce brochure could apply here: "Our most favored asset is a healthy community. Never in its long history has it been marked with intense labor strife. It has no poor residential section. The greater part of the residents being homeowners has been reflected in the beauty of its residential area. It is blessed with many churches, good schools, fine principal services, recreational facilities and cultural advantages, and its proximity to large centers makes available those demands for living not economically possible in smaller centers."

The new New York throughway is about as close to Medina NY as is our Ohio Turnpike. Greyhound bus lines service both cities. They do not have taxi service as we do. They have a full-time fire department, we do not. Each community has ample electric and gas supplies. Our only hotel is no longer a landmark. They have hotel accommodations. Approximately 2,400 dwellings make up residential Medina, NY. About 400 dwellings have been constructed in the city since 1950. Agriculture and related industries form an important part of the Medina-Niagara Frontier. Dairy farming is also a part of their economy.

Surprising as it may seem, although Medina NY is on the barge canal, the only remaining obstacle in the way of industrial progress there is an adequate water supply. Alonzo L. Waters, publisher of the community's only paper said that when a pipeline is completed from the Niagara River, as recently authorized by the state legislature of which he is a member, Medina will be ready for industrial expansion. His words echoed what authorities are saying about our area. The source of water in each case will be the Great Lakes.

Batman

Remember the days of the airshow craze? The days when Mike Murphy, Captain Alex Papana, Danny Fowlie, Jimmy Doolittle, Art Chester and Roger Donre were in the news every weekend? When the Ford tri-motor plane, "Ike" and "Mike," the "Macon" and the "Akron," parachute jumps, gliders, balloon races and aerial aerobatics made headlines in the papers almost daily? Remember the National Air Races, flimsy planes, power dives, dogfights, formation flying and all the other thrills that attracted thousands of spectators to airports, farms and fairs across the country? Remember Merle Auker?

Auker, a Medina high school grad, who learned to fly and parachute jump at Ralph Weinsinger's flying school just south of Cleveland airport on the site of the present Cadillac plant, remembers them well. Auker, now in the contracting business, lives just north of Medina on County Road 141. He has not had anything to do with aviation since his last parachute jump at Montgomery, Alabama in 1941. He looks back on his experience as one he would not repeat again but does not regret. What was his claim to fame in those days?

Merle Auker was a batman. A better name would be a bat-wing parachute jumper. Our high-flying friend first became interested in aviation while still in high school. After some training, he decided that he would not make a very good pilot and pilots were going hungry anyway. Jumpers were doing all right for themselves since there were not many of them and they were in demand at air shows. Pilots were needed too but you had to be very good and very crazy to do what it took to thrill a crowd. Auker did not think that parachute jumping required too much skill and, regardless of what some others may have thought, he did not think he was crazy.

Medina's dare devil Auker's chief claim to fame in those days was his batwing flying. A heavy canvas webbing fastened to his body could be opened by spreading his arms and legs. This permitted him to glide through the air like a bird. A Buffalo newspaper of August 30, 1936 tells the story this way, "For years he had dreamed of soaring through the skies on wings. Now his dream has come true, he thrills thousands with his spectacular exhibitions."

"There is nothing quite like the sensation of free-fall," Auker told your reporter. "It is difficult to explain. During the first couple of hundred feet, I would compare the sensation with that of riding a rollercoaster, after that it is a pleasant relaxing thrill. Paul Gallico, the famous writer once wrote, 'It was a world of imagination filled with fantastic sights not shared by earth-bound humans'. I cannot say that I disagree with that statement either. After all, it took only 15 seconds to drop to where I had to pull the rip-cord and you don't spend much time dreaming if you plan to survive for another trip," he concluded.

Auker's bat-wing rig enabled him to slow his rate of descent from about 150 miles per hour to somewhere around 65 to 90. To spectators on the ground this was an obvious change from the usual rapid drop to the ground. The crowd got a certain thrill out of seeing the human bird soar lazily through the air and Auker's specialty even surprised veteran pilots who watched him perform.

A jumper in those days got up to $75 for a single performance. "I jumped as often as four times in an afternoon which was big money in that day and age," Auker explained. "There was more to it than just jumping. Companies sponsored spot jump contests to see who could land closest to a mark on the ground. There were also delayed drops to thrill the crowd into believing this was a last performance. There were jumps into water, which was easy on the chutist but hard on his equipment. There were illuminated jumps at night, which I did not care for. There was the *cutaway*, which was described by the public address announcer as a tragic accident about to happen since the main chute did not open. I used the emergency chute as planned.

"Finally there were the bat-wing exhibitions. Spot jumping was pretty routine and so was landing on the water, but other jumps had their problems. I used to jump at Chippewa Lake Park every once in a while and Parker Beach would come out in his speedboat and pick me up. A water landing is much better than terra firma but my $425 worth of equipment was subjected to a lot of abuse and I never cared much for that aspect of the job. The illuminated jump was not to my liking either, but not for the reason I mentioned about the Chippewa deal. For the night jump, I carried a spotlight, which I played on the chute when it opened. I am told I looked like a meteor from the ground but from where I was, I could not see a thing. I had no way of knowing where I would land for sure. In fact, I was not sure of that in the daytime.

Once I landed in Rocky River. It wasn't planned that way," he said.

Auker also mentioned that he competed against a dummy in a so-called dummy race. The dummy didn't have a chute but was constructed so that air caught in vent pockets would check its fall. The jumper had to delay the use of his parachute in order to get far enough ahead of the dummy so that when his chute billowed the dummy would not catch up with him before he was on the ground. "The race to the ground was exactly that. Obviously, you could be assured of winning by not opening the chute at all. We preferred to lose rather than settle for the alternative."

"At that time, civil aeronautics authorities had established a level of 2,000 feet at which jumpers were supposed to open their chutes. The 2,000-foot figure, for our purposes, was only an approximation since we had no way of gauging exactly how high we were. Where prize money was involved, we did not pay too much attention to their rules anyway.

"I remember one time at the National Air Races in Cleveland four of us were racing to the ground. When we got down we found out, in addition to the regular prize money, someone was donating two dozen roses with a dollar bill tied to the stem of each rose. That was a big bonus in those days so we were all determined to be first. The next afternoon we baled out at around two miles high. Down, down, down we plummeted closer and closer to the ground past the 2,000-foot, the 1500-foot, the 1000-foot, and the 800-foot level. At 700 feet, the last ripcord was pulled and the winning jumper hit the silk. Boy did we catch the devil from the CAA that day."

Auker's scrapbook clippings revealed a couple of other interesting flying items. One picture showed him landing in the crowded spectator stands at the National Air Races in Cleveland in 1938. Another tells how he made a jump at the Akron Airport in 1936 where strong ground winds blew him away from the field. The article relates that Dan Pelton, a fellow townsman, realized that Auker was not going to drop on the field so he commandeered a car and set out in pursuit. When Auker dropped into a pasture, half a mile from the airfield Pelton was there. He rushed to the rescue and pulled him from his chute.

The young man looked a little shaken so when the official air race car came to take him to the speaker's platform Pelton went along. He was all set to tell the crowd who Auker was and where he came from when Governor Martin L. Davey and his state patrol escort arrived and took over the platform. Pelton said, "If that fellow had just stayed away another minute I would have told the crowd something about Medina." Those were the good old days.

Tony

Tony Kungli, 72, Foote Road, Medina is Hungarian. He hasn't been back to the land of his birth since he came to America in 1907 but he had a few well-chosen words to say when asked about the recent revolution there that failed.

"I came to this country to escape the bossism that existed," he said. "Conditions, no doubt, have changed a great deal since that time but I wonder if my people aren't fighting the same crusade for freedom we so badly needed then? It is true that the Russians have no business in my country. However, if conditions are as bad now as they were then, I would not want to live under either government as compared with democracy. Let me tell you about it.

"I am a mason by trade. At the age of eleven, I went to work at my trade as an apprentice. As an apprentice in those days you received nothing more than board. It was considered an honor to start out the hard way. An apprenticeship lasted seven years. Before the end of my training, as I recall, I was getting somewhere around 50-cents a day and board for my labors. As a skilled craftsman in those days top pay was about $1.60 a week.

"When I became 16 years of age I contracted for my first job. A lawyer asked if I knew of someone who could build him a house. I said I could but he did not know me or what I could do. Therefore, he asked to speak to my parents. My older brother, who was a contractor, thought that I was getting into something I could not handle and my parents were quite concerned. When the lawyer visited the house the following day he asked if they could, or would, furnish bond. When my folks hesitated, he said he was willing to take a chance.

"For completing my first contract I received $150. Of the $150, I spent $75 on the greatest investment of my life; I used it for fare to come to America". Let him tell you about it.

"When I arrived in New York City in 1907 times were anything but good in America. It was not the land of opportunity I had expected to find. I did have freedom, which in itself is worth a lot to those who have felt the confinement of a police state. If anyone can be poor, hungry and happy at the same time, then I was happy. I worked on the East Coast for three years when work was available earning about 45-cents an hour. Then in 1910 I decided to see if there was any better chance of employment in Cleveland. I found that Cleveland, too, was in throes of a depression. We masons needed work so badly that when we saw a cart loaded with brick being driven down the street, we would follow it to ask the boss on the job if he had work for us. There were always more of us than needed, so some earned a few dollars while others went back home to try another day.

"About this time we began to hear that Detroit had plenty of work for everyone. I decided to go there but first my girlfriend and I decided to get married. The following week I left my bride in Cleveland and, after pawning her wedding ring for travel money, departed for *The City of Opportunity*. Sure enough, business was humming in Detroit. Henry Ford was the wonder boy of the era. It was 1911 and his automobile plant was expanding as fast as workers could be recruited.

"I got a job making the great keystone entrance to the main building. One day a fellow came by and asked me to come down from the scaffolding to talk with him. I told him I was too busy and went on about my work. He insisted I stop and I finally consented. He complimented me on the job I was doing and handed me a big cigar. When he walked away others workers rushed over to tell me, I had been talking to Mr. Ford.

"Later in the day the gentleman returned and this time I hastened down from the scaffold to apologize for being so rude. He handed me several more cigars and said, 'People call me Henry'.

"I was so busy I just couldn't find time to get back to Cleveland to see my wife. When I did return she thought I had left her for good. I did not want to leave her again so I stayed in Cleveland and never returned to Detroit. After I had been back for several weeks I received a letter from Mr. Ford telling me that if I were sick and needed a doctor's care he would send the money to me. If I were single he asked that I consider coming back and if I was married, he said money would be available to bring my wife with me. We stayed in Cleveland, I started a contracting business that grew through the war, and everything went well until 1929.

"I had built 30 duplexes on Alexander Road just before the big depression. When it hit, I was only able to salvage enough property on Riverside Drive to trade for a 200-acre farm on Smith Road here in Medina County. Now, of course, things are different. I have a nice house and my boys are well established in the contracting business.

"Wages today of over $3.00 an hour are a far cry from the 50 cents I first earned. Sure this is the land of opportunity. Things have changed much since I came here but certainly no one can deny that our living standards are better than we ever dreamed they could be," Tony concluded.

"In your trade as a mason do you think our mass production and emphasis of speed is sacrificing quality?" I asked. Not at all was the reply. "We had poor workmanship then and we have it today. We get things done faster today because we have better equipment and more know how. For example, in the old country we used to take three months to lay up walls for a 30x30 building. Today it can be done in three hours. If the work was done with pride then it will probably be standing for many years to come, If the work is done with pride now, it too, will last many generations. Our profession is made up of men who take pride in their work just as a tailor or artist does. Those who do not do good work cannot survive long in a field as competitive as building is today."

Jockey Willie

"Horse racing today is big business. Back in the old days it used to be a sport," this is how Willie Jones expressed his feelings about the business that was his bread and butter until just a few years ago. Operator of the shoeshine parlor next to the Medina Theater, Willie has spent 48 of his 50 years around some of the biggest and smallest racetracks in the country. For most of the time, he was a jockey but when the going got rough, a track job was better than none at all. As Willie tells it, horses and racing are a colorful past time. "Some days you make good money and some days you have to settle for what you can get as an exercise boy."

Our friend started working around horses when he was 10 years old. His father had been a jockey and a trainer. One of Willie's first jobs was walking 'hots' or, in our language, cooling off a horse after a race by walking him. In those days, 25 cents was the usual pay for the effort.

"Most people think that horse racing is a crooked business but I didn't find this to be true. Sure, once in a while somebody tries to pull a fast one but they always get caught," Willie explained. "Most of my races were for small purses from $700 to $800. I was a small guy. For each race that I ran I usually got $10. If my horse won, I took home about 50 bucks. I was no Eddie Arcaro, believe me. He's got a big name and he gets big money but I wasn't in that class, no siree," he said.

Willie would race in the North in the summer and South in the winter, which is SOP in the racing game. He even spent some time in Mexico where racing is only allowed three days a week but where derby day, A Sunday, is a big event south of the border. California and Canada were two favorite places for racing. California paid good money for out-gate training riders and for exercising horses in the morning. Canada paid a bonus for place and show riders, something which is not done in the states.

It was a bad fall in Montreal that ended Willie's career in 1953. He returned to New Orleans where he was born, had an operation to get back in shape and then went to work for horse owner Mack Hursh as an exercise boy at Belmont Park, New York.

In 1955, he went to Hursh's farm at Columbia SC, but age had slowed him down and he decided it was time to get away from the tracks all together. "A jockey is a colorful chap that is a good rider, doesn't weigh much and likes horses. If a jockey has these qualities he has some essentials but like many other businesses today he has to also have money, at least he has to have it to start with.

Few people realize the original investment that has to be spent for riding equipment," Willie pointed out. "For example, this whalebone, a riding whip in layman language, cost $30 and was made in England. You can buy *bones* that are more expensive but they do not do any better job. Now take this skullcap-we wore them long before ball players thought about such things-about $10 to $15 is what they cost. Then you need racing boots. The cheapest available today will run about $27.50. You must have exercise pants, socks and underclothes too, and they do not come cheap.

"The biggest expense is saddles, yep saddles. You are right, all you need for one horse is one saddle but saddles are made different weights and you must have more than one in case you need a light one to make your weight or a heavy one to do the same. About four saddles should be enough but at $125 each, you don't start out with a full set. If you don't ride some winners you don't end up with a full set either," Willie explained. The lightest saddle I have weighs 18 ounces. That's not much leather between the horse and me but it's enough.

"What don't I furnish when I race? Well, only the colors. They are the shirt and cap colors an owner has for his stable, like red and white or blue and gold. Some people call them silks because the are usually made of silk.

"Do jockeys make good money? Some of them do but whether they do or not, they spend freely. Sometimes you have to walk a *hot* or exercise a horse just to eat. I would say most of the boys around the tracks do not eat very well, to tell you the truth.

"Discrimination around the tracks? No sir! However, I will tell you this, you have a hard time getting a license occasionally. Licenses cost money too. No license, no racing. How much? Oh, anywhere from $10 up to maybe $20."

Willie weighs 101 pounds and stands four feet eight inches tall. At 58, he has muscles in his legs like those of a high school athlete. But Willie is tired of the track and all the excitement and moving around that goes with it. Sometimes 'the boys' ask him to help them with their racing form choices or invite him to the track. "I don't want no part of the track anymore. If I go once, I will just get started hanging around them again. I don't want that."

Willie is retired. Now he runs the shoeshine parlor on West Liberty Street. It is a quiet, slow business and he likes it. Furthermore, Willie is as proud of a good shine as the man who walks out of his shop with the shoes. He does a nice job and his customers have no complaints.

We interviewed Willie Jones last week while he was home recovering from a bout with pneumonia. "They thought I had tuberculosis but I knew it was a cold in my chest that settled around my crushed ribs hurt in the accident. The doctors told me to stay home for a month so I won't be back in the shop 'till the first of February."

As we said, Willie is a tough little guy. He was back on the job two days later.

Canary Yellow

At 313 North Court Street, Medina is an 86 year old house which has taken on a new look. The freshly painted, bright yellow residence is set off with green shutters and an old-fashioned white steel picket fence. Green shrubbery around the front porch contrasts sharply with the other colors. If it were not for the sign "Antiques" across the front of the house one would be inclined to believe an old-timer had decided to live it up a bit before passing on. Such is not the case. Thirty-six year old Ross Trump has opened a new antique sales room a block North of his other store.

People who think of the antique business as a dusty, moth-eaten barter type enterprise may be surprised by terms like "sales office" and "new look" as used here. They may also be shocked by Trump's choice of colors for his new showplace. They should not be. The antique business is big business today. Something like 40 percent of the buying public will purchase an antique of some kind before the year is over. To handle that volume of sales you have to be almost as conscious of bookkeeping as a supermarket. In fact, the supermarket phase may well be the next outlet for collector items of the past, according to Trump.

Ross got started in the business of collecting things a long time ago for a man of 36. He can still remember the first real antique he retrieved when he was seven or eight years old. He purchased a three-legged stool in a shop in Darrowville. He has not seen a day go by since when he was not thinking about, or looking for, some venerable object out of the past. In discussing material to go into this story Trump, who is anything but a longhair said, "For heavens sake don't sound quaint. This business just is not that anymore, you can study this business in college just as any science. That certainly takes it out of the quaint class."

Obtaining antiques is not a matter of collecting them in some quiet little town like Medina. Because of the development of transportation you may find a worth while piece in a large city where it was taken by someone years ago. American dealers even travel to Europe to bring back Americana that was taken there. European dealers are finding America to be an excellent place to come to for antique items. Many valuable ones were shipped or brought here before the two great wars for safe keeping. It is a dealer's task to get them back into circulation.

Again, because of transportation improvements, there are not many out of the way places that have not been scoured thoroughly. An antique expert watches for items that may be considered commonplace but are highly desirable. Lifting something of a shroud of mystery from the business I asked if old items were obtained by crawling through dark attics and sorting through yellowed papers. "Not at all," replied Trump. "I never go from door to door like a peddler. My name is well known in this trade. People who think they have something of interest contact me or contact some other antique hobbiest who contacts me." According the dictionary the meaning of the word "antique" is something old. According to Trump, this is a better explanation than the government's, which puts an 1830 date on such items. Naturally, the first radios, first automobiles and even the first television sets are antiques to young people today. Speaking of young people, antiques are no longer of limited interest to just the older generation. More young people than ever are buying antiques for their contemporary homes. Architects and interior decorators insist that a period piece is not out of place in a home furnished with modern décor, if properly displayed.

Getting back to the new shop of Trump's, it is furnished for utility. The kitchen display is of early American items. A bedroom is early American primitive. The bath is furnished with red and blue patriotic antiques including political banners, eagles, campaign tokens and, a little out of the patriotic field, a barber pole. Other rooms show items in logical groups with the exception of the front room, which is a combination storage and display area for a variety of items.

When the landscaping of the grounds around the former home of the late Mrs. Minnie Wells is completed it will have a kitchen garden, side garden and garden house. The room just off the kitchen will be a plant display area. Each of the areas will showcase antiques particularly suited to the location.

As noted earlier, Ross Trump made a very special effort to explain why people in the antique business are not eccentrics who live only in the past. He made it clear that only by knowing the beauty of the past can we appreciate the present and the future. For example, Parma High School authorities were so interested in having students know the past is not all cobwebs and high silk hats that a study hall was furnished, complete in every detail, with authentic 18th century décor, even to the extent of including Windsor chairs. Windsor chairs became popular in area homes.

Pattern glassware is still in demand by antique buyers. Antique piece popularity runs in phases. Early American and French Provincial furniture are especially liked today.

Antiques are also good investments. Their value increases faster than today's stocks and bonds. Maintained in the condition that they were received, they will never depreciate.

What of the future? As long as objects are conceived and old objects become obsolete, there will be a market for them. It is true that with the advent of mass production, it may take longer for an item to disappear but, according to Trump, they will. The Bendix automatic washer was the first of its kind on the mass production market just a few years ago. They are not easy to find today.

The Candy Maker

If you are a warm-blooded soul never apply for a job as a candy dipper. You will not qualify. That's the way Anton Horvath, owner of Tony's Candy Store on the square in Medina, tells it. If it had not been for the high price of real estate in Cleveland, Medina would probably not have a candy store today.

Anton came to Medina from Cleveland 36 years ago. The first location for his business was the old American Hotel. Three years later the shop was set up in the Princess Frock Building where Anton dispensed sweets for 14 years. In 1938 the business was moved to the present location. I had supposed that since Anton was Hungarian, and had come to this country in 1913, he brought his candy making trade with him, but that not the case. Tony came to this country by way of Germany. He was a steel and brass worker then with no knowledge of, or interest in, the candy business.

What about the candy making trade attracted his interest is not clear. but he learned basic candy making techniques from books. As in most skilled trades, intimate and essential knowledge comes through experience. The business went well for Tony. It was expanded until three locations were producing a modest income. Then 10-cent stores began to make inroads and automobiles were carrying people past the shops instead of to them. "We used to catch the theater crowds going and coming but cars changed that," Anton said. "At the same time rent began to climb so I decided to get away from it all and come to Medina.

"The biggest factor in candy quality, aside from the ingredients, is weather. A beginner can memorize *Rigby's Reliable Candy Teacher* from cover to cover but if he doesn't consider the weather he will not have much luck. Detecting a weather condition that requires a change in a candy recipe comes only through experience. Cleanliness is important too. A grain of sugar on the marble slab can be the difference between a smooth cream and a crystallized one," he said.

The process of making candy in a small shop compared with a Goliath is not particularly complicated. Ingredients used can be purchased at any super-market. Sugar, flavoring, corn syrup and chocolate are all common ingredients. During candy season from October to June, Tony prepares 20 pounds of chocolates and 30 pounds of creams. A large mixer is used to prepare the ingredients and then, as you would at home, the mixture is cooked.

The cream is then poured onto a marble slab. Marble is used because it cools quickly and evenly. Steel bars are laid around the edges of the slab to contain the cream. When the candy is for chocolate creams hand dipping is the next step. Mrs. Horvath is the dipping expert in the family. A good dipper can prepare 50 pounds of chocolate creams in two and half-hours. Cool hands, the right consistency of chocolate, and the skill of a surgeon are required to get the proper results in the dipping process. The hands must never touch the cream unless covered with chocolate. The moisture from the hands will cause a leak in the cream which, is not a particularly appetizing thing to see when you open a box of sweets.

As you probably guessed, Christmas and Easter are the biggest blessings to the business. Although Easter is considered a bigger buying time many of the items sold then are novelties, such as stuffed rabbits and plastic toys. Christmas is the top candy holiday of the year. *Sweetest Day*, which is the official annual promotion of the industry nationally, does a good job of promoting the industry, but sales are in direct proportion to local promotion. According to Tony, Cleveland has always been a good *Sweetest Day* city, but Akron, until recently, hardly knew such a day existed.

Is the price of candy high today? I thought so until Tony pointed out that after World War I it was higher. The cost of ingredients, labor and packaging account for the cost of good candies. Like any other item you buy, the price is in proportion to quality. "Speaking of high cost, do you know that I have had a salesman show me candy boxes that cost two dollar for an empty pound container? You can't sell candy for 39 cents a pound if the box is five times that figure wholesale.

"Just don't let anyone tell you this is an easy way to make money. It takes a great deal of experience to really become skilled at the candy making art. It is hard to teach apprentices too. When making candy you just cannot stop during each operation and explain it. You have to concentrate on what you are doing to do it right. A candy maker does not like someone looking over his shoulder as he goes about his work. Maybe it's like writing. If you took time to explain to someone why every sentence was written the way it was, you would not prepare much copy.

"In this business, what a beginner would assume to be a correct formula today might be incorrect tomorrow. Naturally, you have to have some basic information to start with. My son John has copied down the recipes for each of the various candies we make. When I leave the business, he will have the information that will be required if he cares to continue in the trade. His success will depend on his ability to modify the formulas to offset uncontrolled outside factors," Anton concluded.

The next time you get the "sweet-tooth" and buy a pound of creams remember, it isn't just an accident that they look appealing and taste good. A lot of experience, knowledge and pride went into a box of what we simply call candy.

Kip

The first floor monkey, basement airplanes and upstairs maid was too good a story to miss. Sure enough, there was the monkey complaining about the price of bananas when Kip Mone welcomed me into his Brunswick home. The "maid," Kip's wife, was upstairs putting the small fry to bed. In the meantime, I was assured there was a full size airplane, two in fact, in the basement, which would be examined later.

Mrs. Mone, pronounced "Moan" came downstairs after a bit and fixed a gallon of coffee. What ever other faults he might have, Kip said he didn't drink the stuff or smoke either, for that matter. As for me, I consumed a pack of cigarettes and at least a dozen cups of coffee while I listened to Mone's exciting tales. Not that he was one to talk much about himself. He really wanted to talk about the monkey who was putting his two cents worth into our conversation.

Kip is a graduate of Brunswick high school, class of '41. Three years before that he was winning junior aviator model awards. He was so wrapped up in aviation he thought about little else. He never missed the National Air Races at Cleveland and he was one of 16 youths selected out of 500 to work with the ground crews at the big show in 1938. Like many eager young men at the time, with a war brewing, he traveled to Fort Hayes in Columbus and signed up for military service. He asked for Air Corps duty and got it flying with the 8th Air Corps in the South Pacific. It was his dream to participate some day in the National Air Races. The dream was as big as ever when he returned from military service. He became a commercial pilot flying out of Youngstown for the Lombard Corporation and the Troyer Company of Mantua and Burton.

The Midget Flown by Kip was Similar to this One

In 1949 he got the opportunity to make his dream come true. He was hired by Art Williams of Alliance, an engineer for Goodyear Aircraft, to fly an 85-horsepower midget airplane in the Goodyear Trophy Race. There was $25,000 in prize money and Kip hoped to get a share of it. Ed "Slim" Honroth, who was born and raised in Weymouth, was also scheduled to race but he was killed at the Akron Airport while flight-testing his entry. The tragedy did not deter Kip. In preparation for the big race, he entered a number of smaller shows throughout the country.

The day of the race came and in some circles, Kip was a favorite. Out of the 25 entrants he had the second highest qualifying speed of 181.603 mph. Bill Robinson of Pacoimz,

California had the number one spot with 183.326 mph. The course was 1¾ miles long. Three pylons were at each end of it to allow wider turns than the year before when two were used. The first race was Saturday. Four eliminations were held. The first and second place winners from each heat moved to the Monday finals. Kip won his first race at an average speed of 173.047 mph. Of the $25,000 prize money he pocketed $320. He was set for the big finale. First place would pay $7,000, not bad for 12 minutes of flying. All dreams are punctured with reality and young Kip was new at this business. He lost the final race by 5.66 seconds and won another $750. Bill Brennand of Oshkosh, Wisconsin won.

Not dismayed by his loss, Kip decided to enter a big air show slated for Reading, Pennsylvania. He noted that Brennand was also entered. Kip would get another chance to prove he had the fastest midget plane. Upwards of 40,000 people were on hand for the Reading Airport 10th Anniversary show. The weather was cool and clear. The sky was cloudless. There wasn't as much money to be had at this race but $1,000 was not too bad.

Kips plane was idling perfectly as he jockeyed into position, he gunned the mosquito-size plane and it leaped into the air. Before the crowd was on its feet, Kip had passed S.J. Whittman who had finished third in Cleveland. Now only Brennand was between him and certain victory. With only four laps to go Kip gunned the yellow racer past Brennand and, as he crossed the finish line seconds later, he put the midget into a victory roll. It was all over. He had won by 400 feet.

Wait a minute! It was the public address announcer, "Ladies and gentlemen, the winner of the race is Bill Brennand." "What happened?" Kip shouted as he dashed to the judge's stand. "Well young fella, you missed one of the pylons at the other end of the field. You went inside instead of outside. Sorry." Kip had struck out again.

Mone's bad luck did not stop him from competing in other races during the next couple of years. He joined *National Air Shows Inc.* and became a regular in the racing game. In 1952, while flying the air show circuit, he purchased a historic *Nieuport* which still had 1917 World War I markings and patched bullet holes in the body. The plane had been used in Hollywood for the filming of *Hell's Angels* and *Dawn Patrol*.

The *Nieuport* was the plane the French sold to us for our American Air Corps squadrons. Many aviation experts believe it was the most beautiful airplane of World War I. It is also remembered as the fighter plane flown by Captain Eddie Rickenbacker's *Hat in the Ring* squadron. Kip flew the ancient "flying rock" as it was known, all over the country for air show demonstrations. It was featured in many airplane model magazines and was on the front page of *Air Trails* in November of '51.

Not satisfied with flying one of the smallest planes in the air, and owning one of the oldest, Kip volunteered to act as a dummy for an air show in Youngstown. He posed as the oldest women in the show, purposely fell out of a *Piper Cub* as it did a slow roll, parachuted to the ground, and was "rescued" by the airfield ambulance to the delight of 25,000 spectators. Two years later, in 1951, he was hired to manage the Chardon Airport. In 1955 he became a corporate pilot for *Thompson Products* in Cleveland, his present employer.

Last year he sold the *Nieuport* for $1,800, the same price he paid for it. He later learned it had changed hands several times and is now back in Hollywood being used to film *Lafayette Escadrille* for $200 a day. When he disposed of the *Nieuport* he bought two antique *Aeroncas* which had been stored in a barn in Mantua.

The low-wing sport plane came off production lines in Middletown, Ohio in 1936. They were so far ahead of their time they did not sell well at the $5,000 price tag. It is these two planes Kip has in his basement. The best parts from each are being used to restore one air worthy *Aeronca* in two sections. When ready for assembly they will be taken across the street to the *Neal Shepherd Auto Agency* where they will be put together. A 90-horsepower *Le-Blond* engine will be rebuilt to power the plane. Completed, the *Aeronca* will be worth a small fortune on the antique market. Kip has organized *American Aircraft Exchange* to broker this and other antique aircraft.

That brings us up to date on Kip Mone's varied and interesting activities. This started out to be a story about the monkey. With all due respects to the critter, you surely agree, it would be hard to match his escapades with those of his owner.

Story Hour

It started one early spring of 1949 at Berrien Springs, Michigan. Stanley Hill, a quiet unassuming man in his early thirties, was walking along musing over the fact that young children of the community didn't seem to be learning child guidance training taught in the church, school or home. What they were being taught just didn't seem to register and he wasn't convinced that it was any fault of the children. Then like the breeze that ruffled his hair as he walked along, Hill said ideas began to pinprick his taughts. As each one would hold his attention for an instant, he would muse over its potential value. None seemed worthy of a second review except one which filled him with enthusiasm. If children could be made to understand the principles that the Bible reveals all their troubles would disappear like magic. Why not present Bible stories to them in a true-to-life manner? Why not arrange for a story hour at the local library on Sunday afternoons? Why not help the young people to grow in character as well as size?

The response to his Sunday afternoon story hours was overwhelming. Someone on the staff of the closest radio station in Benton Harbor visualized that children of the area would like to hear the program, so the station offered free time to the much surprised Stan Hill. A radio show required a scriptwriter and they were hard to find, particularly those who would volunteer their services for nothing. However, Virgil Isles, a student at Berrian College, became interested in the project and offered his talent free.

The basic format of the show, as he envisioned it, should remain story telling. Sam would become Uncle Dan and someone would have to be found for the part of Aunt Sue. Uncle Dan and Aunt Sue would call children together each week for their story hour. The children too, would add their talent to the program by singing songs, reading original poetry or telling about their good deed of the week. Interest in the program spread like wildfire. In a matter of weeks, volunteer help to appear on *The Story Hour*, or to assist with its production, was being offered by children and adults alike. Other radio stations were offering free time just to get the program on the air.

About this time, Ray Hausted of the *Hausted Manufacturing Company* was invited by his friend to Barrien Springs to see his new religious volunteer enterprise. Hausted was amazed by the accomplishments of the amateur group in such a short period of time. He offered to support the program in whatever way he could.

Sometime later, Aunt Sue asked to be relieved of her role in the program because it was taking more of her time than she had anticipated. Betty Hausted had worked with the story hour group since her father was first invited to observe the program and was considered an able replacement. She was finishing college at the time and her training in speech and radio was excellent preparation for such a production. She accepted the job and became Aunt Sue number two.

Requests for program transcriptions began to arrive daily at the *Good Deeder Club* headquarters as well as letters of interest from children and adults. *The Story Hour* staff decided to make tape recordings of their programs so that they would be available to anyone who wanted them free. Some stations and networks all over the country were presenting Saturday or Sunday *Story Hour* programs

A request came in from Australia followed by inquires from Alaska, Newfoundland and Canada. Radio Ceylon, the most powerful radio station in the world scheduled weekly half-hour programs. The quiet library program for children had expanded to a world full of friends and listeners numbering in the hundreds of thousands. A *Good Deeder Newspaper* became another outlet for spreading the good deed principle throughout the world. Prizes donated by friends were sent to children who wrote the best letters telling of their good deeds. Now 175 radio stations are presenting weekly programs. In one week one station recently received 5,000 letters from Story Hour listeners.

Today *Your Story Hour* requires a full-time seven member staff to handle the ambitious enterprise. Two engineers, a production manager and his assistant are required to handle the technical details of the program. Betty Hausted Ahnberg is program director and Virgil Isles, the originator of the program format, is still scriptwriter and producer. Stan Hill, the idea man, still takes the part of Uncle Dan and helps with programming in general.

Many volunteers, some now teenagers, who started on the program as children, help make the tape recordings, handle the mail and perform office tasks. Within three weeks, *Your Story*

Hour will be moved to Medina. Ultra-modern, soundproof studios are now under construction in the basement of the Hausted building at 525 West Liberty Street.

The tape recording programs are sustained, that is to say, supported by the radio stations rather than commercial sponsors. The programs are presented as a public service and are non-denominational. As soon as the studios are completed here, the public will be invited to visit them and to help in program preparation. *Story Hour* people have found that most of their best talent has come from inexperienced children and adults.

Peace, Good Luck, God Bless